D0205461

Pascal Garnier

Pascal Garnier was born in Paris in 1949. The prize-winning author of over sixty books, he remains a leading figure in contemporary French literature, in the tradition of Georges Simenon. He died in 2010.

Emily Boyce

Emily Boyce is in-house translator for Gallic Books. She lives in London.

Praise for Pascal Garnier:

'Garnier's take on the frailty of life has a bracing
originality.'
*Sunday Times*

'Bleak, often funny and never predictable.' *Observer*

'Action-packed and full of gallows humour.' *Sunday
Telegraph*

'Grimly humorous and tremendously dark … Superb.'
*Figaro Littéraire*

'Pascal Garnier is not just an accomplished stylist but also
an exceptional storyteller … *The Panda Theory* is both
dazzlingly humane and heartbreakingly lucid.' *Lire*

# Moon in a Dead Eye

Pascal Garnier

Translated from the French

by Emily Boyce

Gallic Books
London

This book is supported by the Institut français du Royaume-Uni
as part of the Burgess programme.

www.frenchbooknews.com

INSTITUT
FRANÇAIS
ROYAUME-UNI

A Gallic Book

First published in France as *Lune captive dans un œil mort* by Zulma, 2009
Copyright © Zulma, 2009
English translation copyright © Gallic Books 2013

First published in Great Britain in 2013 by Gallic Books,
59 Ebury Street, London, SW1W 0NZ

This book is copyright under the Berne Convention
No reproduction without permission
All rights reserved

A CIP record for this book is available from the British Library
ISBN 978-1-908313-4-92

Typeset in Fournier MT by Gallic Books
Printed and bound by CPI Group (UK) Ltd, Croydon, CR0 4YY

4 6 8 10 9 7 5 3

*Une poussière dans l'œil*
*et le monde entier soudain se trouble.*

*A speck of dust in your eye,*
*and the whole world's a blur.*
Alain Bashung and Jean Fauque

LES CONVIVIALES:

THE RETIREMENT VILLAGE EXPERTS

*Les Conviviales offers a fresh approach to retirement, allowing you to spend an active life in the sunshine. Here's a taste of what you'll find at Les Conviviales:*

A SECURE GATED COMMUNITY

*There's nothing quite like knowing you're protected and secure. With a dedicated caretaker-manager on site 365 days of the year, our residents can enjoy total peace of mind.*

Martial compared the photo on the cover of the brochure with the view from the window. It was raining. It had rained almost every day for the past month. A slick of water shone on the Roman-tiled roofs of the identikit ochre pebbledash bungalows, each fronted by a matching patch of Astroturf-green lawn. At this time of year, the regimented rows of broom-like shrubs provided neither leaves, nor flowers, nor shade. All the shutters were closed. The fifty or so little houses were lined up obediently on either side of a wide road, with gravel paths leading off to each home. Viewed from the air, it must have looked something like a fish skeleton.

HOMES BUILT FOR YOUR COMFORT
*Our single-storey houses are designed with accessibility in mind. Each comes with a sun deck, patio garden, fully equipped kitchen, ergonomically designed bathroom, two stunning bedrooms …*

Aside from a few family heirlooms that had still not found their place, Odette had seized the opportunity to furnish the house with a whole new set of furniture which, by accident or design, bore a curious resemblance to the contents of the show home they had looked around a few months earlier. Martial could not get used to it. Everything had that box-fresh, plastic smell. Fair enough, it was practical, everything worked as it should, but it was like living in a hotel. Odette, meanwhile, was colonising the place with missionary zeal. She could not go into town without bringing some useful or decorative object back with her: a bath mat, a vase, a toilet-roll holder, a hideous black and yellow ceramic cicada … The only territory she had conceded to him was a corner of the cellar for his workbench and tools. This was where he had spent most of his time since the move, working under the lamp sorting screws, nails and bolts by size and storing them in little boxes, which he labelled and stacked on shelves. It was a monotonous task, but he found it soothing.

THE CLUBHOUSE
*The clubhouse provides a place to get together and take part in all kinds of activities. It's where everyone meets to chat, play chess, surf*

*the internet, have a game of snooker, enjoy a cuppa, make pancakes
… Our friendly and helpful social secretary puts on competitions,
walks, day trips, visits to local places of interest and evening
entertainment.*

For the moment, it was closed, and they had not yet met nor even
caught sight of the social secretary. Not that Martial was overly
concerned. In fact, he was somewhat dreading the opening of
the clubhouse. He had no desire to take part in pancake-tossing
competitions with people he didn't know.

SOLAR-HEATED SWIMMING POOL
*Take a refreshing dip in the pool. What better way to relax while
keeping fit?*

The pool was empty. A few centimetres of rainwater stagnated
on the bottom.

YEAR-ROUND SUNSHINE
*All our villages are located in the south of France to make the most
of …*

'As if!'
The catalogue landed with a dull thud on the smoked-glass
coffee table, whose gilded feet were shaped like lion paws.
Martial locked his hands behind his head and closed his eyes.
Suresnes, the Parisian suburb they had called home for more
than twenty years, now seemed like a lost paradise. All those
years spent doggedly accumulating a thousand little habits from
which to spin a cosy cocoon of existence, on first-name terms
with the newsagent, butcher and baker, going to the market on

a Saturday morning and taking the Sunday stroll up to Mont Valérien ... Then, one by one, their neighbours had retired to the Loire valley, Brittany, Cannes ... or the cemetery. The area had changed almost overnight, before they had a chance to notice. A different demographic. Where once peace and quiet had reigned, now screaming children ruled the roost. After months of putting up with Odette nagging him about moving to a gated, sun-soaked retirement village, he gave in. They went to look around the show home in early September. The weather was glorious.

'Just think, Martial, it'll be like being on holiday every day of the year!'

Monsieur Dacapo, the estate agent, had plenty of charm and the gift of the gab. Martial and Odette exactly fitted the owner profile the property company was seeking. Both were retired professionals with a suitable monthly income. The sale of their house in Suresnes would provide a more than adequate deposit. They had no dependants and no pets. Monsieur Dacapo had smoothly reeled off all the retirement community's advantages: security, above all, with intruder-proof fences and strategically located CCTV cameras, and of course the caretaker-manager, whom he made sound like a cross between a bodyguard and a guardian angel. Work on the site was not yet complete but their home would be ready to welcome them in December. Of course, they could go away and think about it, but they shouldn't take too long to do it. A thousand visitors had been expected at an open weekend for a similar village the previous year, but in the event three thousand had turned up!

The deal had been wrapped up in the space of a month during which Martial felt he was going about his life under hypnosis, signing papers he had not even read, carried along by Odette's gushing enthusiasm.

As the first residents to move into the village, they had spent the past month in total solitude. Aside from Monsieur Flesh, the caretaker-manager they sometimes bumped into at the gate, they saw no one. Flesh was a strapping fellow, but didn't have much to say for himself. He seemed to be very good at his job, but he wasn't the sort to slap on the back or have a glass of beer with. Judging by his accent, he was from Alsace, or Lorraine. The tight lips of this timid Cerberus had parted just long enough to let Martial know that another couple was due to arrive in March or April.

Martial stood up and rubbed the small of his back. This new armchair was a waste of space. He should have put his foot down and kept the old one, which had moulded perfectly to his body over the years. Its replacement was stuffed so tightly that when you stood up, it looked as though it had never been sat on. Through the window, the row of TV aerials stretched off into the distance like crosses in a cemetery. *We've bought ourselves a plot to lie in …*

He heard Odette's voice calling up from the cellar.

'Martial, what are you doing?'

'Nothing. What do you think I'm doing?'

'Come down here.'

They didn't actually need to shout; the bungalow was a good deal smaller than their detached house in Suresnes.

'Look, I've made room for the ironing board. I just need you to put a few shelves up, here and here.'

'OK. We'll need to get some wood and brackets … and wall plugs – I've run out.'

'We could go now, it's only three o'clock.'

'If you like.'

'I'll get the stuff to make jam at the same time.'

'Jam? You've never made jam.'

'Precisely, it's about time I started. I found an old cookbook. Now we're living in the country, I'm going to start making my own jams. It's far thriftier that way.'

'In the country, in the country … With what fruit? There's nothing but apples at this time of year.'

'Well then, I'll make some nice apple jelly.'

'Up to you, if that's what you feel like … Right then, I'll measure up for the wood and we can get going.'


Martial pressed the remote control three times, but the entrance gate refused to open.

'What's wrong with this thing?'

'Beep the horn. Monsieur Flesh will let us out.'

At the second attempt, they watched through the fan-shaped patch of glass cleared by the windscreen wipers as the caretaker sidestepped puddles to reach them, holding a jacket up over his head. Martial wound down the window.

'Afternoon, Monsieur Flesh. I can't seem to get the gate open; perhaps there's something wrong with my remote?'

'No, it was the storm this morning. Must have blown the electrics.'

'Ah …'

'I called the management. Someone's coming to look at it this afternoon but I'm not sure what time.'

'And it can't be opened manually?'

'No. It's for security. If you need something urgently, I can get it for you; I'm parked the other side.'

'No, thank you, that's kind of you. If you could just let us know when it's fixed.'

'Of course. Have a good day.'

They spent the rest of the day like two grounded children, sitting in front of the TV until dinner time, which they brought forward half an hour to get it over with. Afterwards, there was nothing they wanted to watch, so they had an early night. As he turned off the bedside lamp, it occurred to Martial that, apart from the dull glow of the caretaker's lodge, there would be no lights on for miles around. They held each other very tightly.

Everything carried on in much the same way until 23 March. The weather had perked up a bit, now raining only every other day. They had on three occasions taken advantage of these temporary reprieves to head into town and to the coast, since the gate had, of course, been repaired. The beach was deserted. They walked along it effortlessly, light-headed from the wind which carried them further and further on. They felt fighting fit. The way back, on the other hand, proved much harder work with the wind against them. Bent double, brows beaten by spray, blinded by the sand flying up in their faces, the soggy trudge seemed to go on for ever. When they finally made it back to their car, their heads were pounding, their eyes bulging, their hearts thumping to a samba beat. It was several minutes before either of them could speak. The wind had played them a siren's song as they set out, a swan song on their return. The experience left them uneasy, with a lingering sense of having narrowly avoided catastrophe. They had not been to the beach since.

The shelves above the ironing board were now firmly in place and had even been adorned with a pretty trim of Provençal fabric – the perfect finishing touch.

New knick-knacks had appeared, like the wrought-iron floor

lamp bought for a small fortune from a gypsy artisan, the ultra-modern transparent plastic magazine rack, not to mention the nightmarish painting of a storm-battered schooner. It was not advisable for sufferers of seasickness to look at it for more than thirty seconds.

Otherwise, they filled their time with TV and books, like convalescents. They had come up with a game, 'the neighbours game'. Monsieur Flesh had twice confirmed that another couple would be moving in shortly. No, he didn't know their names, nor where they came from; 'people like you, I expect'. They didn't know what to make of this ambiguous comparison. What did he mean, people like them? The question had set them imagining their future neighbours in all manner of guises, much to their own amusement.

'Their surname is Schwob. He's tiny and she's huge.'

'They're black.'

'Vegetarian.'

'They've been to China.'

All of which meant that well before their arrival, Monsieur and Madame Sudre's neighbours were no longer complete strangers; in a sense, they were already living alongside them. The anticipation grew by the day, as though Christmas were just around the corner. Then the long-awaited moment finally came, and that day, there was no watching TV. A huge lorry sporting the logo of Breton Removals drove past on the dot of 9 a.m., preceded by a metallic-grey Mercedes coupé which perfectly matched the colour of the sky.

Odette was clearing the breakfast table and Martial was poring over the classifieds in the local paper, his latest hobby.

'Oh, here they are!'

Martial looked up from his newspaper and turned to the window where his wife stood holding the breakfast tray, as though in some kind of trance. The lorry and car pulled up on the other side of the road, right at the end, down by the swimming pool. It was one of the days when it wasn't raining, which meant they could actually see the new arrivals. They watched them getting out of the swish car, the woman surprisingly young, going by her figure at least, blonde-haired and wearing skinny jeans; the man tall and thin, dressed in a brightly coloured tracksuit. He even had hair. Black hair, very black. Martial saw a slight twitch at the corner of Odette's mouth, always a sign she was annoyed in some way. He put his arm around her shoulders.

'See, you can imagine all kinds of things, and something altogether different turns up.'

'They look very young to be moving in here.'

'Well, they're quite far away ... We'll have to wait to see them up close.'

'We should go and introduce ourselves.'

'Yes, but not right now. We'll go over later.'

Now that they could picture their neighbours, however roughly, their efforts to uncover their identities were redoubled.

'Profession?'

'He must be ... a dentist or a surgeon, something medical.'

'Why?'

'He looks the sporty type, fit and healthy.'

'Being fit and healthy doesn't make you a doctor! What about her?'

'Hairdresser, no, perfume counter. Some kind of saleswoman, anyway. Your turn.'

'He ... Oh, I really don't care. We'll find out soon enough.'

'Rubbish!'

'It's true. Now that I've seen them, I've lost interest.'

'Liar! You lose. You're doing the dishes … Martial, come and look! They've got a piano!'

'A piano?'

'Yes, a white one. I just saw it go past.'

'A white piano … Who do you think plays it, him or her?'

'I thought you weren't interested!'

'I know, but a piano changes everything, a white one especially.'

They spent the rest of the day coming up with many and varied contradictory theories about the instrument, which had taken on the status of a third person in their eyes. There was one point on which they were agreed: there was no way you could play classical music on a white piano.

'We should probably introduce ourselves before it gets dark, shouldn't we?'

'Yes, you're right. I'll get changed and we can go over.'

'We're not going to a cocktail party. You're fine as you are.'

'You must be joking! I don't want them taking me for a slattern. I'll be down in five minutes.'

Twenty minutes later they were walking arm in arm up the road towards the heart-warming sight of a house with its lights on. There was something a bit strange about all these houses that looked the same, though; it felt like ringing their own doorbell. The man answered. As the door opened to reveal a stack of boxes in the hallway, the neighbour's lips parted to reveal two rows of unnaturally white, straight teeth.

'Hello?'

'Oh, good evening, um … we're your neighbours, the house over there with the lights on. I'm Martial Sudre and this is my wife, Odette.'

The man's smile, which seemed already to be stretched to its limit, went off the scale.

'What a pleasure to meet you. Maxime Node and … Marlène! … Marlène, come and meet our neighbours!'

Madame Node's girlish figure appeared at the end of the hallway, but as she walked the few steps to the door with her hand outstretched before her, she gained the full weight of her years. She was still slim and trim, but the spots on her skin (which seemed to have undergone a facelift or two) made her look like a withered reinette apple.

'Oh, how kind of you to come! Marlène. How do you do?'

It was extraordinary how Maxime Node could talk whilst still displaying his dazzling array of teeth.

'So, you were the first ones here?'

'That's right, somebody had to be.'

'And … do you like it?'

'Oh yes! It's so quiet! The weather hasn't been great but that's down to the time of year.'

'Of course. Anyway, it's been rotten weather everywhere this year.'

They engaged in the customary small talk for a quarter of an hour, all the while studying each other closely out of the corners of their eyes, like naturalists examining a newly discovered species.

'… and there are so many interesting places to visit around here – churches, the beach … Anyway, we can tell you all about it another time, we don't want to keep you – we know what it's like moving house! Well, have a good evening, and if you need anything at all, just ask. We're the house with the lights on, over there.'

'Great, see you soon!'

Martial and Odette walked back holding hands, like two children coming home from their first day at school. Odette seemed relieved.

'You were right, we had to see them up close. That woman's at least seventy.'

'He's no spring chicken either. That raven-black hair doesn't fool me for one minute, or his teeth for that matter!'

'They seem like nice people though. Smiley.'

'Him especially! My word, he's a walking advert for his dentist!'

'Martial!'

They fell through the door in fits of giggles and, for the first time, the house felt warm and cosy, lived in. They opened a half-bottle of champagne and a tin of foie gras.


The sky was undeniably blue, not a wisp of cloud on the horizon. Though there was still a chill in the air, making an extra layer essential, Martial and Odette had decided to have breakfast on the deck. It was 16 April and the first time they had eaten outdoors. Martial was doing battle with his *tartine*. The homemade apple jelly was too runny, spilling out of the holes in the bread as he spread it.

'So, what do you think?'

'It's nice, very nice. Maybe a little bit runny …'

'That's because of the apples. I could only get Golden Delicious. We're happy here, though, aren't we?'

'Right.'

'They said on the radio this morning it's raining in Paris. Do you realise how lucky we are?'

'Yes … Damn it! I've got it all over my bloody trousers.'

'Are they your new ones?'

'No.'

'Here, wipe them with this. So, what did you make of it?'

'Of what?'

'The drinks at the Nodes', obviously!'

'Oh, it was all a bit fancy for my liking. All those little sweet and savoury nibble things, they're too fussy. I like simpler stuff.'

'I don't mind it every now and then. They certainly didn't hold back on the champagne – we must have drunk at least two bottles!'

'Three! Maxime opened another just before we left. I think Marlène had a few too many …'

'I was a bit tipsy too. I didn't make a fool of myself, did I?'

'I don't think so. I was falling asleep by the end.'

'It was well before then! I had to give you a nudge, you were snoring on the sofa … That sofa! It's …'

'Pachydermic!'

'Exactly! All real leather – must have cost an arm and a leg. But it's far too big for that sitting room. With the piano behind it, you can barely move. I'm not saying they haven't got nice things, but it's all a bit showy. They're the same themselves, very nice people but they always have to go one better, with their holidays, and their friends in high places, and their son the lawyer …'

'We still don't know which of them plays the piano.'

'We don't, do we?'

Inspecting the scrawny shrub, whose branches reached upwards as though imploring the sky, Martial came across a single bud the size of a boil.

Since the Nodes had moved in, Martial and Odette had given up playing 'the neighbours game'. There was no point now that they could get it all from the horse's mouth, without even having to ask. The neighbours crossed paths almost every day, running errands for each other and sharing restaurant and shopping tips. Martial and Odette's superior knowledge of the area made them seem pleasingly like trailblazers, the old hands of Les Conviviales. Piecing together what they had gleaned from all these conversations, they now knew that Maxime had spent his career selling greenhouses all over Europe; that Marlène had danced at the Paris Opéra in her youth; that before coming here they had lived in Orléans and that their son, Régis, was an exceptionally gifted lawyer destined for high office in the near future.

'He's always been able to pick things up just like that!'

Whatever the topic of conversation, Marlène always found a way to turn it to her genius progeny, so that her audience ended up despising the man without ever having met him.

Yes, they were a bit showy, with their clothes, their car and their furniture, but their hearts were in the right place and they were good fun, him especially. He was a real charmer, using and abusing his magnetic smile. He always had a joke up his sleeve and seemed at ease in every situation. In other words, a true salesman. As for Marlène, for all her fragile bird-like demeanour, she was no spare part. She knew her role like the back of her jewellery-laden hand, scolding her husband when his jokes went too far, acting the dizzy blonde when it suited her and always laughing in the right places. All in all, they were pleasant company. No one said they had to be intellectuals. As neighbours went, they were just fine; Martial and Odette could have done much worse. Going their separate ways the previous evening, the two couples had agreed to make a joint visit to a nearby château which was supposed to be very beautiful. Luckily they had not fixed a date for the outing, for which Martial was now thankful. A dinner a month was about enough socialising for him. Plus, it was one thing getting on well as neighbours, quite another to turn that into a friendship.

'Martial?'

'Yes?'

'I was thinking it might be time to get a new dinner service.'

'What for?'

'For having people over, obviously!'

'Like who?'

'Like the Nodes, for starters. We'll have to return their invitation. There's a little shop under the arches. We could head over there now.'

Monsieur Flesh always carried tons of things on his belt: keys, a mobile phone, a torch, pepper spray, a knife; he was a walking hardware shop. He was leaning against the gate smoking a cigarette and staring intensely at the empty sky. Martial slowed down as he drew level.

'Morning, Monsieur Flesh! Beautiful day, isn't it?'

'Very nice, yes. Oh, there's a new person coming, a woman.'

'A woman on her own?'

'Yes. Next week.'

'Right … Well, have a good day, Monsieur Flesh.'

'And you, Monsieur Sudre.'

Sunshine was streaming through the windscreen. After all those months of grey, their eyes struggled to adjust to the riot of colour, as though emerging from a dark tunnel into bright daylight. Odette put on her sunglasses. Her mouth twitched with irritation.

'Something wrong, Odette?'

'No, nothing ... Bit strange to have a single woman coming, isn't it?'

'Not really. She might be a widow.'

'Yes, that's true, she might be ...'

Standing in front of the bathroom mirror wearing only his underpants, Maxime was striking toreador poses. Chest puffed out, belly sucked in, fists clenched beside his hips, he held his breath for long enough to tell himself he still looked pretty good for a man of his age. Then he slowly exhaled, not entirely convinced. As his muscles relaxed, the skin sagged on his hunched skeleton like an oversized garment. He shrugged his shoulders and began to shave.

'Here, at least ...'

All of this was down to a heart scare, a teeny tiny one, but a warning sign. The doctor had told him he had the heart of an ox. But he couldn't push his luck, he wasn't thirty any more. Drinks parties, good wine, good food and ... all the rest of it would have to be reined in from now on. Nothing too serious. But it had been the last straw, hastening their decision to leave. Marlène had leapt at the chance. She had been thinking about it for some time, for other reasons. They had been burgled three times in recent years. The residential neighbourhood of Orléans where they had lived for many moons had become a prime target for the scum who came in from the outlying boroughs. Nothing could stop them, not the most sophisticated alarm systems or the patrols that took place day and night. They were everywhere and nowhere, gnawing away like vermin at the foundations of the stable, quiet life people had worked hard to build. The city centre had not escaped unscathed. Marlène had been mugged in broad daylight at the cash point next to the post office. It took her six months to get over it. Through a friend in the police, Maxime had got himself a firearms licence. His revolver only left his glove compartment at night, when he slid it underneath the bed. They could not go on like that. So it was a combination of things that had brought them to Les Conviviales. He couldn't really complain about the place; it was new, clean, empty of both past and future. The problem was it would soon be filled with nothing but old people. *Old* old people, not like him. People like the Sudres, for example. They must have been about the same age as him and Marlène but, come on, there was no contest … Very nice people, nothing was too much trouble, but could he imagine seeing in the New Year with them? Not likely! And as for wearing socks with sandals, dear God!

Maxime rubbed aftershave into his cheeks, chuckling at the memory of Martial's feet before his expression turned to a frown. There were white hairs at his temples. He would have to get some more dye.

'This is very kind of you, Monsieur Flesh. I couldn't have managed it on my own. If you could put it down there on the deck … a little to the left … There, perfect! Thanks ever so much.'

'You're welcome, Madame Node.'

'It's an olive tree. It'll do well in that spot.'

The fragile stem clinging to its stake, peeking up like a periscope from its huge pot, perfectly summed up the touching pathos of human hope. Monsieur Flesh shook his head doubtfully. The man lacked imagination.

'I'm planning to put a bay tree the other side. What do you think?'

'Better wait and see ...'

'Indeed ... It's funny, my husband spent his whole life selling greenhouses but he hates flowers. Not like my son. He used to make me such lovely posies, even when he was very little! He has a natural eye for it. Do you like flowers, Monsieur Flesh?'

'I look after them. Right, I'd better swing by number twelve. There's a woman coming next week.'

'A woman?'

'Yes, a single woman. Have a good day, Madame Node.'

Marlène took off her brand-new gardening gloves and watched the caretaker walking back up the road. His arms dangled at his sides, as though pushing an invisible wheelbarrow. A single woman ... Well, she had to be old in any case. And anyway ... He would never admit it, but since his heart scare, Maxime was not quite the same. Something had changed, imperceptibly. It was as though he felt he was being watched. He was always checking the time; it had become a sort of tic. It couldn't be down to her; she had given him free rein years ago, leaving him to his own devices so long as their life together was not disrupted. She had realised early on this was the only way to go. She did not resent him for it, it was just the way he was – he liked to feel attractive. And he had attracted her, so much so that she had left the Opéra to focus all her attentions on doing the housework. She didn't regret it;

she would probably never have made it to prima ballerina. In any case, she had never gone without; Maxime was generous and had showered her with enough luxuries to allow her to forget the essentials. And then Régis had come along ... You were allowed to have your children to stay for two weeks of the year here. She had already got his room ready ... Maxime had got angry ... She had cried ...

An ant emerged from between two flagstones. Knitting its antennae together, it seemed to ponder which way to go. Marlène crushed it under her foot.

Odette felt like learning something, but she wasn't sure what. Italian, ikebana, yoga, belly dancing, Turkish cookery, surgery – anything, as long as it was new! So much time on her hands … Every day felt as long as a Sunday. This was her time, hers and no one else's, and she could do whatever she liked with it. Yet the vast virgin territory bestowed upon her was no more than a big lump of ice floating on an ocean of emptiness, melting a little more each day. It preyed on her mind, the fear of wasting it. She wasn't used to such freedom, and felt burdened by it. She had done as she was told her whole life, not simply out of laziness or lack of courage, but because she sincerely believed that modelling her existence on a train timetable would put her on the right track for success in the workplace and at home. It might not be perfect, but she had yet to discover a better alternative. There was cinema day, mountain-hike day, the day they went for dinner at so and so's – and life was good … or so it seemed to her.

Odette took off her glasses and rubbed her eyes. A gust of wind ruffled the pages of the interiors catalogue lying open on her knees.

She wasn't so certain any more. But what was the use in dwelling on the past? All that mattered was the here and now. They were both in good health, they had everything they needed to be happy, and they were free!

Her gaze followed the line of the security fence which screened off her horizons. A ray of sunlight bounced off the black eye of a CCTV camera.

There was no reason to doubt it, they had been happy, with a few ups and downs, the odd regret, but nothing worth stewing over! They had lived an honest life. The world had become cynical; nobody took these sorts of values seriously any more. Well, if the world had moved on from them, they had moved on from it too. She and Martial were perfectly capable of looking after themselves – they'd been married forty years after all! And it had gone without a hitch! They hadn't even needed to have children; the two of them got on just fine on their own. There was no reason for that to change …

The shadow of a doubt was obscured by the sun for a moment. Everything became a uniform grey, cold and silent, like during an eclipse. Odette shivered, not only from the chill but something else, a sudden feeling of lacking, an emptiness that took her breath away. Then the sun came out again. She heard the reassuring hum of the TV from the living room. The Nodes waved to her as they drove past. It must be around midday. Everything was getting back to normal.

'Martial?'

'Yes?'

'Don't you think we should call Dacapo about the clubhouse?'

'What for?'

'To get them to open it, of course! I mean, we're paying for it, aren't we?'

'There aren't enough of us.'

'Excuse me, there are going to be five of us soon! We're entitled to it anyway. I don't know about you, but I want to do things.'

'What things?'

'Well, I don't know! That's for the social secretary to think of. It's her job to come up with things for us to do.'

'Fine, we'll call him. Let's heat up that gratin, I'm hungry.'

'Did you hear that thing on the news, Martial, about a doe attacking an old lady?'

'It was a roebuck.'

'Yes, well, same thing. I mean, bears, yes, wolves even, but a doe? I don't know what kind of muck they're spreading on the fields these days. All the little creatures guzzle it up and then go mad. You'll see, soon it won't be safe to walk anywhere.'

They were having a drink on the deck at the Nodes' place. The two women were indoors. You could hear the low murmur of their voices, the occasional word or burst of laughter ringing out clearly. It had not yet quite become a ritual, but they were going round to each other's houses more and more often, and the mood was ever more relaxed. They had a good time, talking about everything and nothing, especially Maxime, who always had something to say whatever the subject. He found silences oppressive and was compelled to fill them. This suited Martial down to the ground, since he had spent his life cultivating the art of making conversation by nodding and smiling in agreement. Yes, it was nice, watching the sky turn mauve, then from mauve to purple, the stars coming out unnoticed. They had good weather almost every day now. Everywhere they looked, it was turning green. Everything they touched was sticky. Spring was in the air.

'Top-up, Martial?'

'No, I'd—'

'Go on, let your hair down!'

'OK then, just a drop.'

Martial and Odette hardly ever drank, even with dinner. They had had to stock up in time for the Nodes' first visit and since then, Martial had not been averse to the odd glass when the opportunity arose, as it did more and more often. It had not escaped Odette's notice, and she had brought it up with him recently. Well, he was hardly going to become an alcoholic at his age. There was no harm in loosening up and letting that warm fuzzy feeling come over him now and then. Odette took those pills every night, after all ...

'And what about this black beast that's been seen prowling around the dunes near Calais? They're saying it could be a panther. Did you see it on telly?'

'The photo the police showed wasn't very convincing. It looked more like a large cat.'

'Judging by the paw prints, they reckon the animal weighs about eight stone. That's one hell of a moggy!'

'Do you know the Côte d'Opale?'

'No. I know the Basque coast very well though. I spent six months in Biarritz in '56 ... no, '57. That was the life! One night, at the casino ...'

Martial sucked his ice cube. The Côte d'Opale, the dunes studded with with marram grass which scratched at your calves, the cliffs, the wind ... Wissant, between Calais and Boulogne,

where he had spent his holidays as a little boy … So long ago
… He would go out fishing for crabs and winkles with Nicole,
a girl of his own age from Lille … Back then, he had no idea he
was destined to spend his life behind a desk – he wanted to be
a deep-sea diver when he grew up. It had been centuries since
he last visited Wissant, even in his thoughts. The beast in the
dunes took him back. It must have changed there too, no doubt
about it … At low tide you could walk along the beach for miles
with your eyes closed, without bumping into anything at all …
Straight ahead …

'What do you mean, "straight ahead"?'

'I'm sorry?'

'You just said "straight ahead".'

'Did I?'

'Yes.'

'Sorry, I must have been daydreaming out loud.'

'That's all right. One more for the road?'

'No, I won't, thank you.'

'If you're sure … So, she'll be here tomorrow!'

'Who?'

'The newcomer, of course, the single lady.'

'Oh yes, that's right.'

'What do you think she'll be like?'

'I don't know. Odette thinks she's a widow.'

'How funny, that's what Marlène says too! She could just be
divorced.'

'Or she might never have married.'

'Exactly! Why do they insist on her being a widow?'

'I don't know. Maybe the thought reassures them; it implies
someone respectable and dignified.'

'Dignified? Please! I knew a widow in Limoges, by God, she was a feisty one! Listen to this, one day I got back to my hotel and …'

After casting a furtive glance towards the house, Maxime leant close to his neighbour's ear. Martial could not stand people sharing these sorts of secrets with him. They brought out the same feelings of shame and disgust as when he saw his first porn magazine. Thankfully, Odette and Marlène chose that moment to come out onto the deck and Maxime pulled away with a wink, holding a finger to his lips.

'We all know women like to gossip, but look at the men! Martial, have you seen the time?'

For the past week, Odette had been trying her hand at exotic cuisine, cooking anything and everything as long as it originated from the other side of the world. Distance seemed to be a key ingredient in the recipe. On the menu that evening was that dish Mexicans went wild for, chicken cooked in chocolate. She had spent most of the afternoon making it. Martial sat back while Odette served him, keeping his mouth shut. It looked like *coq au vin*, but smelt like a dessert. He took a mouthful. Though his taste buds had had a few days to adjust to their culinary world tour, his tongue was immediately on fire.

'Don't you like it?'

'No, I do! It's just very hot …'

'Maybe I put a bit too much ginger in.'

'No, it's fine.'

'What were you talking to Maxime about?'

'This and that … animals.'

'What about the widow?'

'Come on, Odette, why are you so set on her being a widow?'

'Why shouldn't she be? Anyway, Marlène agrees with me.'

'And what does that prove?'

'Women can sense these things.'

'Oh, right! Look, I really couldn't care less. We'll soon find out one way or the other.'

'We will, won't we?'

Martial woke up with a start in the middle of the night. It was not a nightmare, more a sense of having forgotten something important, like turning off the gas or a switch ... something vital ... It had something to do with the dunes at Wissant ... At least, he thought it did ... His throat raging, he got out of bed to fetch a glass of water and was amazed, looking down, to see his erect penis straining the fabric of his pyjama bottoms. In the kitchen, he swallowed one of Odette's pills with his water.

Léa took one last walk around the house before turning off the lights and going into her room, where she fell back on the bed, arms outstretched.

'My final resting place ...'

She had never pictured it like this. She didn't know whether to laugh or cry. Madeleine had always been generous towards her, but with this bizarre gift she had ensured her dreadful taste would live on after her death. That said, Léa would not have been at all surprised if this unlikely inheritance (the house and a comfortable pension) had been somewhat cynically arranged by the family of the deceased, all too happy to see the back of the *very* personal assistant to the owner of Lomax pharmaceuticals. Madeleine would have signed anything at the end. It was only right to provide for a faithful ... employee. Perhaps if she had pressed the solicitor to look more closely at the will, Léa might have got more out of it, but what was the point? There was nothing else she needed now.

Good old Madeleine ... Perhaps she might have preferred to end her days here herself, rather than in her mansion on Paris's

Avenue de Wagram. She liked the simple things in life: going for walks, watching TV, eating stews ... That was pretty much all they had done together for the last few years, yet they were both contented. Each of them had looked back at her own life and realised that past a certain age, independence begins to feel like a trap. What they had never amounted to love, but the arrangement they had come to many years before had fostered a tenderness that was something like it.

Léa rolled onto her side. She felt acid rising in her throat. It must have been those red-hot fritter things Madame Sudre, Odette, had served.

She had been a little taken aback to find the four of them on her doorstep. The removal men had only just left and she had barely had time to get her breath back. They stood there smiling like Jehovah's witnesses, the tall one especially, Maxime Node. He was the one who introduced everybody, showing them off as though trying to get a good price for them. Then they had all begun talking at once, each of them impressing on her their willingness to help. They didn't seem like bad people, but they still frightened her a bit. Too eager, too smiley, too many outstretched hands ... so old and wrinkled it was hard to tell whether they were grasping or giving. She couldn't turn down their invitation to the buffet party they had put on in her honour at the Sudres', the house closest to hers. The four of them seemed to get on well and to be happy living there. It was strange, but Léa felt straight away as if she knew them, or rather recognised them as people she had crossed paths with long ago, colleagues or classmates ... The clown, the shy one, the flirty one, the swot ... It was always the same. Claiming tiredness after a long day, she managed to escape, though not without assuring Odette of her support on two apparently burning issues: opening the clubhouse and filling up the pool.

'Because, you see, there are five of us, now that you're here. Five!'

Those greasy fritters were not going down well at all. Using a pair of nail scissors, Léa tore open a box marked MEDICINES in the harsh fluorescent light of the bathroom. She dropped two Alka-Seltzer tablets into the tooth glass. She could see the Sudres' window from hers; their light was on too. Her gaze was learning its limits.

'We still don't know if she's a widow or not.'

'And what does it matter to you?'

'It doesn't! I'm just interested, that's all. Anyway, she's a thoroughly decent woman; she agreed straight away about the clubhouse. I'll call Dacapo tomorrow.'

'You do that. Can I turn out the lights?'

'Yes. She must have been very beautiful once.'

'She still looks good.'

'A bit too good. It makes me wonder what she's doing here.'

'What a thing to say! She's come for the same reasons as the rest of us, for the peace and security. It makes even more sense for a woman on her own. And she might want to meet people.'

'What people?'

'Well, I don't know. There'll be others, could be some single men, who knows?'

'You don't get many single men at our age. Good night, Martial.'

'You see, Marlène, that's what I call class, high class even! Well-spoken, well-mannered, but not all la-di-da, not snobbish, just very natural and … classy!'

'If only the same could be said for everyone.'

'And what's that supposed to mean?'

'If you could have seen yourself, poor old sod! Thank God you can't die of shame.'

'What exactly are you getting at? I was just being friendly!'

'A bit too friendly, if you ask me.'

'For goodness' sake, you're not going to go all jealous on me, are you?'

'Not at all. I just think she seems like a very nice woman and I don't want your silliness to put her off us. You need to get it into your head that you're nothing like her type.'

'And what is her type, may I ask?'

'A man with class, that's what.'

'Like your son?'

She was quiet for a moment. 'You're disgusting.'

That had to be it, up on the hill, that pink spot that looked like an army camp. Les Conviviales. Nadine pulled up on the verge and lit a joint, the weed home-grown in her garden between rows of tomato plants. Well, she needed something to buck her up before walking into the lions' den – even if the lions were toothless. Why had she taken the job? Because it was a job, after all, and those didn't come around very often. And, as usual, she was short of cash. What was she going to get these old folk doing? Macramé? Model-making? Silk painting, pasta necklaces? Until now, she had only run workshops for children, plus the odd class for bored housewives. As for the elderly – oops, 'senior citizens' – she didn't have a clue. Calling to offer Nadine the job, Catherine had assured her it would be no more of a pain in the arse than looking after kids; old people moved around less and were worn out more easily. One day a week, 200 euros a pop. The guy Catherine knew from the property company, Dacapo, had called the previous day. He needed someone, anyone, to look after the clubhouse of a retirement village, starting as soon as possible. Two hundred euros … one day a week …

Nadine wound down the window. The thick smoke from the spliff rose up in the air like a wad of grey cotton wool. She sat watching it for a while, the back of her neck pressed against the headrest. She really wasn't looking forward to this. Catherine was always coming up with these half-arsed plans. How many times had she dragged her into some crazy scheme? It was a laugh when they were younger, but now … Nadine would be forty-five next month. She had had enough of dunking small hands into paint pots and clay. It was becoming unbearable. The sight of a child's painting repulsed her. They were all as useless and badly brought up as each other. So really, why not give the oldies a go? Not that they were so much older than her, anyway … It was only one day a week; she'd still have another six for painting her little watercolours and smoking little joints in her little house.

As the hash began to take effect, Les Conviviales, framed by the windscreen, took on the glossy veneer of a postcard. The whole thing looked fake, like a hurriedly assembled stage set daubed with unsubtle colours: blue sky, pink walls, chalky white ground streaked with patches of green. Nadine aired the car for a few minutes before turning the key in the ignition.

Monsieur Flesh eyed Nadine suspiciously, clearly tempted to act the policeman and circle her clapped-out Clio before letting her through.

'And you are?'

'Nadine Touchard. I'll be running the clubhouse. Weren't you told I was coming?'

'Yes.'

'So … can I come in?'

'Yes.'

The gate opened slowly, as though equally reluctant to let the little red car in.

'Could you possibly tell me the way?'

'Straight on, you'll see it, by the pool.'

'Thanks. Have a nice day.'

She had trouble deciphering the grunt she received in response. Caretakers are gruff types. Nadine drove slowly, as though following an invisible funeral cortège.

'Jesus, it's completely dead.'

Bland bungalows ran along both sides of the road like so many polished tombstones; it was enough to make you fear for a somewhat monotonous ever-after. At the end of this ghost road that seemed to go on for ever, the blue rectangle of the swimming pool came into view, and behind it, the chalet-style clubhouse. A small group of men and women were waiting outside. They all stopped talking the minute they saw Nadine's car, and didn't take their eyes off her until she came to join them. It was like a scene from a spaghetti western.

'Hello, my name's Nadine Touchard.'

Five right hands were thrust in her direction, some wearing gold rings or bracelets, all of them crisscrossed with swarms of thick blue veins under sagging, spotted skin. As Nadine shook each one in turn, she felt strangely as though she were offering her condolences.

Everything in the 'leisure centre' was new, from the electric kettle in the kitchenette to the computer, not to mention the snooker table. So sparklingly new that nobody dared touch anything, nor even sit down. Anxious to give the impression she had everything under control, Nadine walked breezily through the building, nodding her approval at the quality of the furniture and equipment that had been provided. The truth was, she was a total technophobe and had never picked up a snooker cue in her life. *What the hell am I doing here?* The others stared silently at her, as though watching the slow, painful death of a fly trapped in a blob of honey. Nadine was beginning to regret smoking that spliff. The silence seemed to press on her eardrums and subliminal images flashed before her eyes. She had to take charge of the situation, and fast.

'Great. What do you say to getting to know each other over a cup of coffee?'

At this, they all seemed to loosen up and the atmosphere instantly became friendlier. Léa and Marlène offered to make the coffee while the others settled into the sofas in the reading corner.

Over the course of two hours, they covered every subject, except the one they were supposed to be discussing. Catherine was right; it was quite straightforward dealing with old people, you just had to go along with whatever they said.

'Isn't that so, Mademoiselle Touchard?'

'Call me Nadine. Absolutely, absolutely ...'

Once she had identified the leaders of the group – Odette Sudre being the serious one and Maxime Node the joker – she could let it run on autopilot. Martial constantly rubbed his hands together, stopping only to surreptitiously pick his right ear. Marlène kept crossing and uncrossing her legs, looking daggers at her husband. And Léa had worn that same lovely little sad smile throughout. She had clearly had a lot of practice at politely putting up with being bored stiff, and Nadine instantly warmed to her. She didn't belong here either. What was she doing here?

Taking advantage of a lull in the conversation, Odette cleared her throat.

'Good, that's all very good. See you same time next Thursday.'

With great solemnity, Madame Sudre closed the folder marked 'Clubhouse'. Inside was a pad of paper, blank but for the page on which she had just written: 'Clubhouse Meeting 9 a.m. Thursday 14th. Agenda: Suggestions for activities.'

They parted beside the pool, chorusing how nice it had been to get to know each other. Nadine got back in her car. Once the gate had closed behind her, she lit a joint and took a long drag on it. The hills rolled ahead of her, as far as the eye could see. She decided to stop by the beach before heading home. She felt a desperate need for space, to feel the wind.

Yes, it was like living on holiday, the only difference being that holidays came to an end. It was as though they had bought themselves a ticket to the afterlife; they no longer had a future. Which just went to show you could do perfectly well without one.

Martial put down his watering can. It was barely nine o'clock and it was already hot. This palm tree looked bloody silly. It reminded him of the office junior at the ministry whom everyone called Gaston Lagaffe after the disaster-prone comic strip character, a long-necked simpleton who wandered around with his head permanently in the clouds. No one could believe it when he was arrested for armed robbery. You never can tell ... It was Odette who had brought the palm tree home from a shopping trip with Marlène. She wanted her own patch of garden to make her mark on and fill with her choice of rare, exotic flowers. You could get away with it in this climate, she said. Some plants died within days, others clung on. It was hard to make sense of. Nature's a funny old thing, it does whatever it pleases. He had always been a little afraid of it. He tiptoed into forests, speaking in a whisper, as though entering a church. Nature was mysterious, incomprehensible, impenetrable, off limits, like the ladies' toilets.

'OK, I'm ready. Shall we go?'

Odette had put a blouse on over her swimming costume, as flimsy and brightly coloured as butterfly wings, along with a white swimming cap and a pair of sunglasses. She was getting quite tanned. It suited her, just like her shorter, newly highlighted hair. They had taken to going to the pool every morning at nine o'clock, 'when it's quieter,' said Odette. 'Quieter ...' It made Martial smile. For the time being, there were still just the five of them, with no new arrivals on the cards. They weren't exactly fighting for space in the pool. In fact, it was starting to feel a bit weird, all the empty houses. Maxime had joked about it the other night.

'What if they're watching us, like guinea pigs in a lab? They could secretly be filming us and studying us like rats ...'

'Why us? There's nothing out of the ordinary about us. We're just normal people.'

'Really? How many "normal" people do you know? Everyone's got a few skeletons in the cupboard.'

'But who would be watching us?'

'I don't know ... Other people, on the other side of the wall ... Martians!'

OK, he'd had a bit to drink, but ever since then, Martial had looked at the CCTV cameras differently.

Odette was the first to get in.

'Come in, the water's lovely!'

No. To him, it felt icy cold. His toes curled around the rungs of the steps.

'Come on!'

He let go. It was like being born, a great big slap in the face. But didn't it feel wonderful afterwards! Martial did a couple of lengths as quickly as he could, so he could get them out of the way. It wasn't to do with the temperature of the water, he just found swimming boring. You never got anywhere and you had to constantly jig your arms and legs about to avoid going under. All around, there was nothing to look at but blue. It was a bloody waste of time.

He was busy drying his hair when Léa arrived.

'Morning, Martial. How is the water?'

'Morning, Léa. It's nice, very nice!'

Léa put her things down on a deckchair and dived in to join Odette. Even though he saw her every morning, Martial still could not get over how attractive she was. Of course, it was plain to see she wasn't twenty years old any more, but her skin was so smooth, not an ounce of cellulite, her chest and thighs so firm ... And the way she walked, standing tall and almost gliding ... You know, she looked even younger than Nadine. Or not younger exactly, but more ... Classy, as Maxime said every time he undressed her with his eyes, leering over his dark glasses. Martial had been surprised to find himself looking at her in the same way, and was disappointed in himself. Léa was not a flirt, she was just friendly to everyone. She was unassuming, hardly ever talking about herself or what she had done in her life. Sometimes she went out early in the morning and didn't come back until nightfall. 'I went for a walk.' Yet she was always on hand to help if someone needed her. She wasn't aloof, and everyone thought highly of her.

Martial closed his eyes and lay back with his hands behind his head, listening to the two women's voices and the little splashing noises.

'I read about this little eleventh-century abbey church in my guidebook, about twenty miles from here. It sounds very interesting. I was thinking it might make a nice day trip. What do you say, Léa?'

'That sounds like an excellent idea!'

'I'll bring it up at the meeting next Thursday. We could set off mid-morning and have something to eat while we're there …'

Then he fell asleep with his mouth wide open, poised to swallow up the sky and all the birds in it.

On her way home, Léa bumped into the Nodes outside the clubhouse. Marlène was wearing a blue and white striped robe and a funny little pointy hat in the same fabric, which made her look rather like a beach hut.

'Morning, Léa, heading off already?'

'I have a doctor's appointment.'

'Nothing serious, I hope?'

'No, just a repeat prescription.'

Maxime muttered a vague greeting, avoiding Léa's gaze. She took no notice.

'Right, see you later then. Have a good day.'

That moron had been sniffing around outside her house the previous night, as she was getting ready for bed. She had just turned off the TV and was closing the curtains when she saw a figure through the hedge that ran along her deck. She thought it must be Monsieur Flesh doing his rounds and had gone out to ask him something. There, crouching behind the bush, Maxime was pretending to tie his shoelaces. She almost burst out laughing at the guilty expression on his face, like a little boy caught stealing from the biscuit tin.

'Maxime? What are you doing here?'

'Me? Oh, nothing, I just came out for a walk. It's too hot, I can't sleep.'

His eyes were bloodshot and he smelt of alcohol.

'Would you like a nightcap?'

'Well, if you're offering ...'

Again she was forced to stifle giggles as he puffed out his chest and sucked in his stomach, his dentures gleaming in the half-light. They sat out on the deck. Léa fetched two shot glasses and a bottle of ice-cold vodka. Maxime could not seem to believe his luck.

'It is hot, though, isn't it?'

'Yes, it's hot, it's summer.'

'Right ... You ... You don't wear a wedding ring?'

'No. You have to be married to wear a wedding ring. Like you.'

'Of course. So you've never been married?'

'No.'

'I see. Mind if I have another?'

'Go ahead.'

As he toyed with the signet ring weighing down his little finger, Léa could sense him planning his next move, like a hunting dog sniffing out a trail.

'It can't be much fun for you, being on your own ...'

'It's my choice. And I'm not on my own all the time, I have friends.'

'Ah yes, friends, I understand. I bet you have a whale of a time, don't you? All the good bits, without the domestics! You're dead right. Freedom's what it's all about. Marriage kills love.'

'Why did you get married then?'

'Oh, it's another story for me. It was such a long time ago ...

Anyway, there are ways of getting around it, if you know what I mean!'

His words were accompanied by such an exaggerated wink that this time she could not help but laugh out loud.

'Listen, Maxime, I don't want you to get the wrong end of the stick. I'm very glad to have you as a neighbour, but you're not at all my type.'

All at once, Maxime's flashing neon smile went dead.

'But ... I don't know what you're implying ... So what is your type?'

'Someone more like your wife than you, if you see what I'm saying. Marlène is a wonderful woman.'

He opened and closed his mouth several times, but made no sound. The wrinkles on his forehead rippled like little waves.

'It's late, I'd better get going. Thanks for the drink.'

It was silly of her to have said it, but how else was she going to get him off her back? He wasn't a bad person, just a little over-friendly. Sloping off down the road, he really looked like an old man.


When she got home, Léa showered, got dressed and filled a large bag with everything she would need for a day at the beach: a book, a piece of fruit, sun cream ... Followed by an ashtray, a cup, a clothes brush, a trivet, and anything else she could lay her hands on. With the bag full to bursting, she stopped in her tracks.

'What on earth am I doing?'

She looked closely at both sides of her hands, then at everything around her, the furniture ... Nothing seemed palpable or tangible; she could be anybody, anywhere. She slumped onto a chair and rubbed her temples.

'Oh God, it's starting again ...'

Maxime was lying on his deckchair dripping with sweat, but he refused to get in the water. He was sulking, and therefore not in the mood for anything. Marlène and Odette were slathering themselves with sun cream, gossiping and giggling like girls; Martial was snoring, blissfully unaware of the alarming shade of scarlet he was turning, and Léa had gone home. What a sorry bunch. They were probably better off without Léa anyway. The truth was he was still reeling from last night's cold shoulder. A dyke, that was all they needed! ... And if that wasn't bad enough, she was eyeing up his wife, yes, drooling over Marlène! ... Just you try it, go on! ... That two-faced ... She looked like butter wouldn't melt. Going around smiling at everybody, passing herself off as a poor lonely widow ... A lezzie, that's what she was! A dirty bloody lezzie! ... The only reason they'd bought this dump was because they'd been assured their neighbours would be of a certain calibre, no one too foreign, no dogs, no cats, no children or grandchildren for more than two weeks at a time ... Well, if they were going to let lesbians in, it would be fairy boys next! ... He had a mind to write to the management, he'd show

them who they were dealing with! ... 'Not her type' indeed ...
What did she know? You couldn't go around judging people, just
like that. All right, looking in the mirror that morning, he knew
he'd seen better days, but that was only because he'd had a drink
the night before ... He'd take up sport again. That's right, he
would go back to playing golf. He had found a nine-hole course
nearby, a bit dated but perfectly decent. The only trouble was
Marlène couldn't play any more because of her arthritis, and he
couldn't be bothered to go on his own.

'Oh, hello, Maxime, I didn't hear you arrive. I think I might
have dozed off.' Martial half smiled drowsily, his face now puce.

'I wonder, Martial, do you play golf?'

As usual, Marlène stopped the car at the gate and began probing the depths of her bag in search of her beeper. Odette sat waiting next to her, watching a fly zigzagging across the windscreen.

'What on earth is he doing?'

Marlène looked up.

'Who?'

'Monsieur Flesh, over there.'

To the left of the entrance, behind a row of spindle trees, they could see him bobbing up and down with a spade in his hand, like a crazed jack-in-the-box. He was not digging but hitting something, over and over again.

'Has he gone mad? ... Oh my God, how awful!'

Monsieur Flesh had just stood up again. He held in his fist the tail of a cat whose head had been reduced to a shapeless, bloodied mass. For a few seconds the two women sat motionless before Odette leapt out of the car, followed by Marlène.

'Are you out of your mind? What have you done to that poor creature?'

'I'm doing my job.'

The caretaker cast an emotionless glance at the remains of the cat before flinging it up in the air, where it followed a smooth parabola before landing in the wheelbarrow with a dull thud.

'Why did you have to kill it? You could have just chased it away.'

'And then it would have come back, bringing another one with it, and then another … Believe me, I know what I'm doing. It's for your own good.'

Marlène was biting her fist, unable to tear her eyes away from the dead creature.

'But really, with a spade …'

'When you do a dirty job, you have the right to do it the dirty way. Have a good day, ladies.'

Monsieur Flesh grasped the handles of his wheelbarrow and pushed it away, without a hint of remorse. Odette brushed a fly away from her face.

'What a brute! I always thought he looked the violent sort.'

'And with a spade as well …'

'I'll bet he'd do exactly the same to a human being.'

'Now, I think you're going a bit far, Odette. I'll admit Monsieur Flesh doesn't exactly seem like the sensitive type, but he's just trying to do his job. We can't blame him for that. Are you an animal lover, Odette?'

'Not especially – I wouldn't club one to death though … What about you?'

'I gave it a try. We got a dog after we were burgled the first time, some kind of sheepdog. We had to let it go; it was biting everybody, even us.'

'Oh, this fly!'

'What fly?'

'It's been buzzing around me since this morning and it's really starting to get on my nerves! It was there at breakfast, at the pool, in the car and now …'

'The same fly?'

'I can tell it is. No question … Right, I suppose we should be off if we're to get those sardines for the barbecue.'

Their faces lobster-red, hair plastered to their foreheads, the four women were cooling off in the clubhouse lounge, sitting around the computer looking at the photos of the eleventh-century abbey church taken that morning. Every so often, one of them would catch sight of herself leaning romantically against a pillar or gazing up at the ogival arches, would bring her hand to her mouth and cry, 'Oh, how ghastly! I'm so unphotogenic.'

Causing the others to reassure her in unison, 'Don't be silly, you look lovely. It's the flash, it wipes everything out.'

The solemnity of the setting had led them all – even Léa – to adopt the same expression reminiscent of a constipated Virgin Mary. Only Nadine wore a wide grin, like a slice of watermelon. It should be said she had twice claimed a need to use the facilities, sneaking out for a quick puff in the chapel courtyard. Even now, her retina was still throbbing from having stared too long at the psychedelic light show of the stained-glass windows, and the other women's voices sounded distant and distorted, as though coming through a tube.

This job was really beginning to grow on her. Of course, it was all a complete con, but at least everyone was getting something out of it ... She got on well with the three women; the two men made only brief appearances, like actors playing bit parts. It was rather like going to visit her aunties for the day. Odette was a born organiser and loved to be in charge. In fact, she arranged almost everything and no one seemed to mind, they were all in agreement. It didn't really matter to them where they went, whether it was an exhibition, a craft market or an abbey church; they just enjoyed spending a few carefree hours in each other's company. What's more, Nadine was being paid for her troubles, which meant she had finally been able to get her toilet flush fixed. As she had got to know them better, she had realised that, leaving aside bank balances and a few years on the clock, there really wasn't that much difference between her life and theirs. Especially Léa, who was single, just like her. Wasn't Nadine's little house, like Les Conviviales, a kind of bunker where she too lived tucked away in her own little world? She had to laugh, really. Having spent years living in a commune, carrying the cards of all sorts of wacky organisations, fighting for countless lost causes, she had wound up so disillusioned that she had said to herself if she could not change the world, she would at least make sure the world did not change her. Had she managed it? It was doubtful, to say the least. In any case, it seemed to her now that these wealthy old people were also misfits of a kind, a species left to ensure its own survival, rebels almost.

Odette switched off the computer with a sigh of satisfaction.

'I'll print off the best ones tomorrow for our album. What a pity Martial didn't come. I wonder how Maxime managed to drag him along to play golf. Martial hates sport ... Damn, missed it!'

She had just slammed her hand down on the clubhouse folder. Frowning, brow furrowed, with her nose in the air, for a few seconds her gaze followed the winding path of a fly only she could see. Ever since 'the cat day', Odette had been tormented by this fly, the very same one. She had told everyone about it but still no one else had actually seen it – except Martial, but he was only pretending.

Marlène stood up, fanning herself with a medical journal.

'When are they going to sort the air con out in here? That fan really isn't up to the job. I think I might go for a swim.'

A wall of heat hit her the moment she stepped out of the door. The pool looked white-hot, as though filled with boiling mercury. Blinded by the glare, she screwed up her eyes and shielded them with her hand.

'Ah, here come our returning champions!'

Maxime's car was making its way down the road, but it was not him driving. The coupé passed right in front of Marlène, stopping outside her house. Martial was behind the wheel, wearing a strange look on his face. Next to him in the passenger seat, Maxime seemed to be trying to climb inside the glove compartment. The four women dashed towards them.

'What's the matter with him? What happened?'

Martial looked like an elderly little boy waiting to be told off, with his baseball cap, Bermuda shorts flapping about his skinny legs and the massive two-tone golf shoes Maxime had lent him.

'He seized up.'

'Seized up?'

'Yes, took one swing and then … crack.'

Maxime was still peering into the glove box, both hands clinging to the dashboard.

'Get me out of here, damn it!'

Taking every possible care, they eventually managed to prise him from the car like a winkle from its shell, and carried him, bent at right angles, to his bed. He looked like a colossal foetus. With tears in her eyes, Marlène stroked his head, saying, 'My poor darling', over and over.

And he replied, 'Blasted bloody stupid fucking game!'

In contrast to him, the others stood perfectly upright around the bed.

'Has he seen a doctor?'

'Yes. He gave him a sedative. I've got a prescription here too for some shots …'

On hearing this word, Maxime tried to pull himself up, which only served to worsen his pain. He hung there speechless, eyes bulging and mouth wide open.

'We'll leave you be. If you need anything at all, Marlène …'

'Thank you, thanks very much.'

They crept outside without making a sound, except for Martial, whose studded soles clattered on the paving stones. Odette shrugged.

'You'd have been better off coming with us, but there you go … Nothing wrong with you, is there?'

'No. I'm just a bit knotted up. I don't think I like golf.'


'Are those the only shoes you've got?'

Martial had looked down at the grey socks and orthopaedic sandals that were permanently attached to his feet.

'No, I've got the ones I wear in town …'

'OK. What size are you?'

'Forty-one.'

'I'm a forty-three. Mine will be all right on you, better too big than too small.'

It was nice driving with the top down. The breeze went to your head, like champagne. Unfortunately, Maxime was going rather too fast, sitting back in his seat, hands in peccary-leather fingerless gloves gripping the wheel, a black and gold leaf-patterned cap perched above his Ray-Bans.

'Churches, pah, honestly! Once you've seen one, you've seen them all. After St Peter's, in Rome ... Have you been, Martial?'

'No. It must be quite something!'

'It's big, bloody huge! There's marble and gold all over the place! You name it, they've got it! Now that's what I call a church! As for this St Whatsisname's Abbey ... who gives a damn?'

The golf course was like a mini Switzerland, a land where nature had finally been tamed by man. The trees had been given a short back and sides; the plastic lining of neat little ponds had been cleverly camouflaged by rows of bamboo and the grass had been perfectly trimmed to three different lengths, from the rough to the green via the fairway. Maxime had explained all this to him while pointing out the various stages of the course with the end of his iron, like a general preparing for battle. A Swiss general, that is, setting out to occupy nothing but his own time.

'And what about those sandy bits over there?'

'They're the bunkers. If your ball lands in there you'll have a hell of a time getting it out again. Best to steer well clear. The red flags in the distance mark where the holes are. Some of them take three strokes, others four or five, depending on the difficulty of the course. Ah! Did you hear that bell? That means the players ahead of us have moved on to the second hole. We can get started. This little plastic mushroom thing is called a tee. I'm going to place it right here and put my ball on top of it. Watch closely ...'

Though he could not put his finger on why exactly, Martial did not feel at ease in mini Switzerland. The golf course reminded him of the extra-terrestrial landing grounds described in the science-fiction novel he had just finished. Ever since Maxime had put that laboratory idea into his head, planting the notion they were all being watched, Martial had begun reading all manner of off-the-wall books which had led him to doubt everything around him. What if those red flags were some kind of signals and the bunkers, the craters left by space ships? And what if Maxime ...

'Martial, old boy, look at me, I'm showing you what to do! ... You hold your club like this, left hand here, right hand there, feet flat on the ground parallel to the direction the ball's going to take. Roll your shoulders back ...'

Martial watched his neighbour whipping his club to and fro over the short grass, all the while wondering why the Martians were so keen on colonising Earth. The whole place had gone to the dogs, you only had to listen to the news to know that. It must be a complete dump where they came from ...

'Right. Now I'm going to show you what a real swing looks like!'

Maxime bent over, wiggled his buttocks and shifted his feet as though stubbing out a cigarette. Then he suddenly lifted the club above his head and struck the ball with all his might. It all happened in the space of a few seconds, the time it would take to draw a comma, or cut off a king's head. The ball flew up in the air, high enough to join other galaxies, while Maxime was left standing twisted as a grapevine, letting out a piercing cry before falling onto the grass in the position he would remain fixed in. Luckily, since they had only just teed off, the clubhouse (yes, there was one here too) was close by and Martial managed to haul Maxime there without too much trouble. Once inside, an off-duty doctor had given him first aid. Well, he said he was a doctor, but his ears were a bit too pointy ...

Léa and Nadine had watched the Sudres walking back towards their bungalow, she a few steps in front with her head held high, he dragging his feet as though carrying some heavy burden. Both women felt the urge to laugh.

'Do you fancy a glass of wine?'

'That would be lovely!'

Léa's house felt strangely like a hotel. Of course, there was furniture, paintings hanging on the walls and expensive ornaments, but nothing gave the impression of having been expressly chosen. The furnishings were only there to fill the rooms. It was a kind of B-movie set on which everything seemed to have been screwed permanently in position. The only things out of place were the clothes strewn about as though a suitcase had just been unpacked. The living room was filled with the scent of melon.

'A nice chilled rosé?'

'Sounds perfect!'

'Head out onto the deck, I'll be right with you.'

Nadine settled into one of the loungers. A bath towel was hanging over the arm. She lifted it to her nose; it smelt of Léa. A single hair caught in the fabric formed an arabesque, like an initial.

The wine was delicious. Léa had brought out cubes of frozen melon which melted in the mouth. The sun was setting. The world seemed to be at peace again.

'Léa, can I ask you something?'

'Of course.'

'Why did you decide to move here?'

'To be honest, it wasn't me who decided. It was ... a gift.'

'Oh ... how funny ...'

'Why is that funny?'

'It's just a bit odd, isn't it? I mean, the person who gave you this ... "gift" must have known you pretty well?'

'Yes, and ...?'

'I'm sorry to be rude, I barely know you, but I don't think this place suits you. It's not your style.'

'Don't you think? It's quiet, comfortable, and I have very nice neighbours ...'

'It's quiet, all right! I've been to graveyards livelier than this!'

'Now, really, it's not that bad ... Perhaps it's not what I would have chosen, but I had no other option.'

'Why don't you sell up?'

'The thought has crossed my mind. I even looked into it, but it's practically unsellable. I mean, look at all these empty houses. And anyway, would I really be better off anywhere else?'

'See, you're talking as if this place was your tomb! What's making you so sad?'

'You know, sometimes I feel like going back to bed before I've even got up. I was sitting out here last night, looking at the stars, and I wished I could pull the sky down and wrap myself in it, and then go to sleep for a very long time ...'

'You're unhappy ...'

'No, I'm not. Why should you have to be unhappy to want to die? Anyway, let's talk about something else. Are you sure you wouldn't like a bite to eat? A bit of salad maybe?'

'OK then. I'll help you.'

The kitchen could not have been used much either. Utensils were kept to a bare minimum and the inside of the fridge was like a wasteland. They began slicing tomatoes and onions as comfortably as old friends. Nadine did a pitch-perfect impression of Odette, while Léa tried to copy Maxime's blinding smile. The wine had made them a little tipsy, breaking the ice between them.

'I bet you have a good laugh at us, don't you?'

'I have to admit it can be hard to keep a straight face sometimes. Like the other day, when Marlène … Léa? … What are you doing?'

Léa was smiling, dead-eyed, while filling the salad bowl with everything that came to hand: vegetable peelings, her keys, her purse … Nadine looked on, stunned.

'Léa, are you drunk?'

Léa did not hear her. Unfazed, she simply carried on adding things to the bowl.

'Léa, are you OK?'

Nadine took hold of Léa and turned her round to face her. She was so vacant it was as though she had been hypnotised.

'Come and sit down. Come on.'

Léa let herself be led to the sofa. No sooner had she sat down than she closed her eyes and fell asleep. She was still smiling.

'It's up to you, but don't say I didn't warn you.'

It seemed to Marlène that Monsieur Flesh, with both hands on the car door, holding his face inches from hers, bore an uncanny resemblance to the dog they had had to part with. He smelt like a dog too.

'Are there … are there many of them?'

'Three or four caravans. But this is just the beginning, there'll soon be others. It's the same every year, always around this time. Honestly, you'd be better off getting your husband to go with you.'

'He can't get about. It's his back …'

'In that case … It's up to you. Anyway, have a nice day.'

Gypsies … Marlène turned back, her forehead creased with worry. What a nuisance, the fridge was almost empty and Maxime had asked her to get him some magazines … It was only 10 a.m. People didn't get their throats cut at 10 a.m. … But Monsieur Flesh seemed to be taking it seriously.

Sitting in his armchair, propped up with cushions, Maxime saw his wife pulling up outside the house.

'Did you forget something?'

'No. I've just seen Monsieur Flesh. They've set up a gypsy camp right by the junction with the main road, you know, that scruffy patch …'

'So?'

'So, he told me it's not safe for a woman to go that way alone.'

'Oh … so what are we going to do? We haven't got any bread, or any … What about my magazines? … Go and ask Martial.'

'Their car's not there.'

'What about Léa?'

'She's gone out too. I saw her leave first thing this morning.'

'Damn it! … Go and get my revolver from under the bed.'

'What for?'

'Just get it!'

Over the past two days, Maxime had not spoken more than a dozen words, and those he had spoken were short and sometimes very coarse. Unable to move from his chair, he sat brooding and staring through the window in the hallway at the nothingness outside. You could almost see the thought bubble hanging above his head, filled with daggers, skulls and crossbones and lit bombs. These gypsies had turned up just at the right moment to become the focus of his hatred for the whole of humanity. They were the ones taking the bread out of his mouth, stopping him reading *Autosport*, lying in wait, with knives between their teeth, to jump out and rape his wife! And of course they would have to come on a day when everyone else just happened to be out. You could never rely on anyone but yourself. Marlène held out the Smith & Wesson he had used only once at a shooting club. Maxime's score had been so pitiful he had never set foot in there again. He checked the barrel was loaded and slid the gun between two cushions.

'You aren't going to do anything stupid, are you?'

'What do you think I'm going to do, stuck in this chair? Push me closer to the window so I can see them coming.'

'See who coming?'

'The gippos, obviously!'

'They can't get in here! We've got Monsieur Flesh …'

'Him! Honestly, darling, what do you expect Monsieur Flesh to do against that lot? They're crafty, believe you me, they've got it all worked out!'

'How's that?'

'How? Well, they'll have lookouts. They will have seen the Sudres' and Léa's cars going past and know we're here on our own. Trust me, they'll grab their chance!'

'But what about Léa … she was on her own … You don't think …'

'How are we to know? … Go and make us a coffee, I think we're going to need it.'


Monsieur Flesh must have been mowing the lawn on the other side of the village; they could hear the motor going back and forth like an insect buzzing persistently. Marlène had managed to throw together some emergency rations of crackers, tinned sardines and tomatoes.

'Can't fight on an empty stomach! Do you know what gypsies eat?'

'No. What?'

'Hedgehogs. That's right, hedgehogs!'

'Makes sense. There are so many squashed on the side of the road … Gypsies, roads, hedgehogs, it all fits.'

'Don't be ridiculous. You get hubcaps all along the road too and they don't exactly eat those.'

'No, they steal them. I've heard they can take a car apart in the time it takes to buy a loaf of bread.'

'Don't talk to me about bread! Thanks to those mongrels we've got nothing but crackers. How are you supposed to mop up your sauce with that? ... Where the hell are the others? It's almost two o'clock! I've got a bad feeling about this. And him, over there, he should stop driving us up the wall with that bloody lawn mower and keep guard!'

'It is getting quite irritating. Reminds me of that fly Odette keeps going on about. Have you ever seen it?'

'Of course not. It's all in her head. Might be the only thing in there ...'

'Why do you have to be so mean? I think she just needs her eyes testing.'

'She always has to have everything her way. I've had enough of it!'

'Why do you care? You never want to join in anyway.'

'No, and it's because of her!'

'I don't believe that for a minute. You've been funny with everyone for ages, even Léa. You can hardly bring yourself to give her the time of day.'

'Oh, you are something else! May I remind you that five minutes ago you were jealous of me getting on too well with her!'

'You just don't get it, do you?'

'Get what?'

'Anything. Do you want to watch TV?'

'No, I do not!'

'Fine. Suit yourself. I'm going to have a nap.'

How long had it been since the two of them had made love,

even badly? So long that Marlène wondered if she really missed it. Every so often an intense rush of desire might come over her, when even a piece of music, a waft of perfume or a certain quality of light were enough to bring her out in a hot flush ... But it would soon pass, like a projector moving on to the next slide. She had never breathed a word of it to anyone and had ended up telling herself it was just a part of getting old. But deep down she was not so sure, now lying semi-naked in the blue light of the bedroom, the heat seeping in through the shutters, beads of sweat forming on her top lip ... Inside her belly, her chest, there was someone fighting to get out of this useless body that had been washed up on the bed, a voice protesting at the imposture, the unfairness of it all. And yet she knew she could still turn a man's head in the street. A real street, obviously, not here where it was a toss-up between Martial and Monsieur Flesh ... She had been in such a good mood that morning, getting herself ready to go into town on her own. What did the gypsies have against her? What had she ever done to them?

In the living room, Maxime was nervously whistling the theme tune of *The Alamo*, the cult western that held the top spot in his cinema hall of fame.

The bullet had whistled so close to Martial's head that ten minutes later it was still ringing in his ear. It was as though Odette's fly had moved in there.

'He's mad! Mad, I tell you!'

On the way back from their walk, Martial had stopped off to give Maxime and Marlène a berry tart, the speciality of a village he and Odette had visited that afternoon. He was about to push open the garden gate when the shot rang out. For several seconds he stood frozen, the only movement his eardrum vibrating like a tambourine, endlessly replaying the sound of the gun going off. The tart, loosely wrapped in paper, slid out of his hands, landing on the white flagstone like a scarlet cowpat. He slowly took a step backwards, then another, until he reached the middle of the road, where he turned and broke into a sprint. It felt strange to be running, like having his whole body picked up and shaken. Other than hurrying to catch a bus or a train, he had not run anywhere in decades.

Martial had arrived home breathless, deathly pale and incapable of either stringing two words together or controlling the shaking in his legs. Odette sat him down and tried to get him to drink a glass of water. He managed only two mouthfuls; his teeth were chattering too much against the glass. Once he had finally prised his tongue from his palate, he gave a jumbled account of his bizarre brush with death.

'But why would he have shot at you?'

'I don't know! I told you, I was just about to open the gate, like I always do, when ... A gun going off, the bullet, a scream ... all at once.'

'A scream?'

'Yes ... there was a scream from somewhere in the house, from the same place as the shot ... But it was me being fired at, I can still hear the bullet ...'

Odette let go of his hands. He was shaking so violently that she in turn found herself vibrating from head to toe.

'He must have gone mad ... unless it was someone else ... not Marlène ... Look, that's her running over here now! ... What on earth is going on?'

No sooner had Odette opened the door than Marlène flung herself at Martial's feet, sobbing.

'You're not hurt, Martial?'

He stiffened, his jaw clamped shut, and shook his head. Marlène clutched her chest.

'Thank God, oh thank God! It was an accident, Martial, he made a mistake. It wasn't you Maxime meant to fire at.'

Odette stood between them, raising an eyebrow.

'Who did he mean to fire at then?'

'The gypsies.'

'Gypsies? What gypsies?'

'The ones camped out by the junction with the main road. Surely you must have seen them ...'

'A gypsy camp? Did you see any gypsy camp, Martial?'

'I don't think so ... Oh, actually there were a couple of caravans ... So, what about them?'

Marlène picked up the abandoned glass of water from the table and finished it in one gulp, before patting her chest.

'I'm sorry. Well, I was heading out to the shops this morning. We had nothing to eat in the house. I saw Monsieur Flesh at the gate and he warned me about this gypsy camp. He seemed to know a lot about it; he said they come back every year and it's not safe for a woman to go near them on her own. The thing is you've no choice but to stop there to give way to the main road. He seemed like he really meant it. So I turned back and told Maxime what had happened. You weren't home, neither was Léa; we felt ... vulnerable on our own. Maxime thought they might take advantage of the situation to try something, so he got out his revolver. If only I could tell you how sorry he is now! Even more so since the kick from the gun put his back out again. Please come back with me and tell him you won't hold it against him ... He so wants to say sorry ...'

Maxime had had to buck himself up before facing the music. He had made serious inroads in the bottle of Scotch sitting beside him. His voice thick, he set the scene of the drama once again.

'You see, I'd been sitting here waiting for them since this morning and I must have nodded off for a minute. I heard footsteps coming and started opening my eyes, but you had the sun behind you, Martial – I couldn't tell it was you! I shot into the air, just to scare them off – obviously at such close range, if I'd wanted to hit them ... And then, crack! The most excruciating pain went through my shoulder and down my back, as though I was being snapped in half. You see, a gun like that has a hell of a kick to it! ... Anyway, everyone's fine now. That's all that matters.'

Maxime downed the rest of his drink and clicked his tongue. The silence crackled, like champagne quietly fizzing in a flute. Marlène stood up and looked out of the window. It was dark outside.

'Everyone except Léa. Her light's not on.'

Martial could not tear his eyes away from the gun lying on the table, which now looked as banal as a piece of cutlery. Odette cracked her knuckles and got to her feet.

'Now look, I think we should all try to keep our heads. It's only nine o'clock, this isn't a boarding school. Léa can come and go as she pleases, whatever time of the day or night. As for these gypsies ... We went straight past them and nothing happened to us. I didn't even notice them.'

'That's the point! You obviously don't know much about gypsies. They're masters of disguise. You don't see them, you think everything's peachy and then, bam! You end up with a knife in your back.'

'That's a bit over the top, Maxime.'

'Not at all, Odette! I served in the war; I know a thing or two about ambush ...'

'You fought against the gypsies, did you?'

'No, of course not! But they're all the same ...'

'Who's all the same?'

'Other people! The ones who are out to get us and take our things! Oh for Christ's sake, forget it. If you'd rather shut your eyes to it and let them cut your throat while you sleep, that's your problem.'

Marlène grabbed the bottle and moved it out of reach.

'That's enough, Maxime, pull yourself together! I'm sorry, Odette, it's his nerves.'

'It's fine, I understand. Look, we're in the safest place imaginable: we've got CCTV cameras, an electric fence … and Monsieur Flesh! You saw what he does to cats, so I think we can all sleep soundly. As for Léa, I'll say it again, she's a free agent. If she's still not back in … a while, then perhaps we should think about raising the alarm. Don't you think, Martial?'

'Absolutely.'

'Marlène?'

'I … I don't know. Maybe. Either way, I really must do my shopping tomorrow.'

'We can go together, don't worry. Maxime, I think you should put that gun away.'

'You do what you think best, Odette, but I'm keeping my eyes open, and if I were you, Martial, I'd do the same, whatever your wife might have to say about it.'

Odette shrugged, waving her hand in front of her nose. Did this fly never sleep?

Martial watched the war coverage late into the night. There was nothing else on. Odette had been asleep for ages. He turned off when they announced the cease-fire. Nothing much was happening by then.

'... the rumble of shelling died away and silence fell ... The only sound was a bird singing, the wind in the trees ... It's ... overwhelming. Back to the studio.'

He had sat watching the same old pictures of war-torn buildings standing white as bone under a blue sky, windows blown out, riddled with black holes; diggers sifting the debris; people covered in dust wandering, crying, bleeding and beating their chests, their faces streaming with tears and sweat. Others were chanting unfamiliar words, war talk, and making 'V' for victory signs. Both sides did the same, as though everyone had won. They wore filthy jeans and ripped T-shirts, scarves around their heads, and bearded faces all blending into one.

This new breed of war always seemed to take place in perpetual sunshine. Following the example of OAPs, war had decided to retire to warm countries. Never Norway or Finland. He had seen

a man lifting up the body of a newborn baby. A day-old child …
twenty-four hours … What must he have made of his short time
on Earth? … Twenty-four hours, with bombs raining down …
He wasn't bleeding; he was like the porcelain figurines hidden
inside *galettes des rois*. War was not scary when you watched it on
TV. You could tell yourself the world was under construction.
They were building bridges. All the time building bridges, linking
up roads to nowhere, roads that dwindled into the desert. You
were never quite sure where all this was happening. Somewhere
far away. Martial preferred the night footage, when fluorescent
green fireworks exploded across the screen.

But for now, they had stopped fighting. Worn out, they had
called it a day: to be continued. Shame, he didn't feel like going
to bed. He poured himself a glass of ice-cold milk with orgeat
syrup and took it outside to drink under the stars. It would be
hot again tomorrow, even hotter than today. They were calling it
a heat wave on the news and warning the elderly to drink plenty
of water and keep to cool rooms. The sky had rarely seemed so
vast to him, nor so full of stars. There was hardly any black left.
One great big moth-eaten curtain, a lacework of lies. If only you
could press your eye against the cloth and see what lay beyond.
There might be nothing there but light – who could tell? The
24-hour baby probably, but given the circumstances, he had
decided not to stick around to let us know. Why did it have to
be such a big mystery? We'd all spend a lot less time agonising
over it if we only knew for sure. There's nothing beyond. Why
couldn't they just tell us that, rather than filling our heads with
their terrifying tales …

A satellite was trying to forge a path through the sizzling stars.
It looked so pathetic, a struggling starlet … He almost wanted to
wave his handkerchief at it …

Martial had never gone to war, though he had served his time at the Naval Ministry in Paris. The position was not without risks; he might easily have died of boredom. But he had never fired a gun, never killed anybody. He was proud of the fact, but at the same time would have liked to know what it felt like. He had never raped anybody either ... There seemed to be a lot of fornication in times of war. Everyone was so afraid, they clung to what they had, with fear in their bellies. And of course it was dark, everyone was hiding in cellars and they had to find something to do to kill time ... By having sex, they could push death away, resist it, and make 24-hour children ....

It was almost a full moon. Maxime could have played golf on it, there were just as many holes and bunkers ... Maxime must have killed people, raped them too no doubt ... He would have to ask him how that felt ... The bullet that had whistled past his ear had left behind the echo of a secret, the whisper of a revelation. What if it wasn't as bad as all that? ... If it was OK to ...

'Martial? You're still up?'

'Yes. Too hot.'

Odette, crumpled with tiredness, Odette with lined cheeks, Odette just the way he loved her, laid bare, his constant other self. It was a good thing she had woken up because this concave sky, graffitied with untranslatable hieroglyphics, was starting to scare him.

'What are you drinking?'

'Milk and orgeat.'

'That sounds nice. Fancy another?'

'Please.'

The satellite had disappeared to the other side of the world, while the stars carried on calmly grazing on nothingness. The other lounger creaked as Odette lay down on it.

'It's twenty-eight degrees in the kitchen. Who knows what it'll get to tomorrow … Martial, what are you thinking about?'

'Nothing. Lots of things, it's hard to say … I'm happy we're together, here, you and me, and not dead yet.'

'Is this because of the bullet?'

'Could be … Have you seen the sky? It's amazing, isn't it? It's like the big top at a circus …'

They held hands. They weren't scared of anything any more, felt like crying a little, or laughing.

'What happened to the fly?'

'Shut up, it's asleep … Oh look, there's Léa coming back … She's absolutely fine …'

Armed with a long-handled net, Monsieur Flesh was clearing the swimming pool of the insects that had come to drown there during the night. Without interrupting his slow circuit of the water's edge, he nodded at Léa and immediately turned away. He was wearing nothing but khaki-coloured shorts and a pair of flip-flops. His body gave off an unsettling aura of brute force. Everything about him was hard: the expression on his face, his close-shaven hair, his muscles and his refusal to talk. Solid as a block. Léa set down her canvas bag and laid her towel over a deckchair, took off her sunglasses and made her way to the steps leading into the pool. It was barely nine o'clock and the water was already lukewarm. Léa let go of the rails and flung herself backwards. It was like putting on a second skin: cool, supple and soft. She lay floating on her back with her eyes closed, lulled by the gentle lapping of the waves that rippled around her body at the slightest movement. She was revelling in the sensation of dissolving into the water, when something floppy brushed against her shoulder. The contact with her skin stunned her like an electric shock. She felt her whole being recoil. Thrusting her hips to pull herself upright, she took in a mouthful of water and spluttered. She threw her head back, flicking the hair from her face. Through the water streaming over her eyes, she saw Monsieur Flesh looming above her, silhouetted against the dazzling sunlight, holding his net up like a trident.

'My apologies.'

He stood absolutely still, like a bronze statue staring blankly at her, eyes devoid of all expression. Again, he muttered, 'My apologies', before pulling the net towards him and carrying it away over his shoulder.

Léa got out and grabbed her towel. No matter how hard she scrubbed, she could not shake off the unpleasant sensation of the mesh brushing against her skin.

'He did it on purpose ...'

She suddenly felt very lonely. It was as though the world had ended, and she was the last to know. She lay down on the lounger and closed her eyes. The Sudres should be here by now ... As keenly as she had wanted to avoid her neighbours yesterday, she now desperately missed them. The episode with Nadine when her mind had 'gone blank' had really shaken her up. She had opened her eyes to find the younger woman sitting beside her, a look of deep concern on her face. Of course, Léa could not remember what had happened; she never could. She had tried her best to reassure Nadine that she would be OK. It was just something that came over her now and then, a funny turn, nothing serious. All she had to do was take her tablet and she would sleep like a baby. Nadine could go home; there was nothing to worry about. It was so kind of her to have stayed and looked after her, thank you, thank you ... Left alone, she had sat outside waiting for the first light of dawn, her mind still full of the nothingness that had all but engulfed her.

She had headed into town first thing and, after wandering aimlessly for a while, had come across a brass doorplate which read: Dr F. Glaive, GP. No, she didn't have an appointment. Yes, she could wait. Three others were already sitting in the waiting room: a young woman with a little boy of six or seven, and a shrunken old man, squashed into the chair like a stubbed-out cigarette. Léa took her place among them, whispering a soundless 'Hello' which met with a similarly low-volume murmur in reply. Apart from the child swinging his legs under the chair, everyone was stock-still, like ornaments on display. The dark wooden panelling, the smell of beeswax and the stuffy, silent atmosphere made it feel like being shut inside grandma's dresser. The mother gave her son's leg a sharp slap.

'Will you stop jiggling about!'

A regular rattling sound rose from the old man's chest, fading into a high-pitched whistle as it passed between his cracked lips. You could hear the dust falling, and see it dancing in the ray of sunlight filtering through the frosted window panes. The cannibal minutes fed on the silence. Léa felt a growing urge to cry out, to release some kind of primal scream. She stood up abruptly, left the waiting room, made her way down the long corridor, mumbled a few words of apology to the receptionist and tore down three flights of stairs. Leaning back against the heavy carriage door, she breathed the street air deep into her lungs; despite the whiff of sewage and petrol fumes, it seemed miraculously pure.

She wanted to eat something, drink something, laugh out loud. At a nearby tea room, she ordered a cup of coffee and a madeleine. Yes, a madeleine, that was just what the doctor ordered!

Afterwards, she treated herself to an expensive pair of shoes, along with a sackload of useless trinkets that seemed essential. She lived the whole day in the moment, or rather, in a series of moments, each fading away as another took shape: exchanging a few niceties with a German woman in a restaurant; flicking through a newspaper on the beach; watching a seagull flying in a corner of the sky; looking at the film posters outside a cinema; hearing them say on the radio, 'There are 50,000 roundabouts worldwide, with 25,000 of them in France alone'; the smile of the supermarket checkout girl, the feet, so many feet pounding the pavements, a face in the crowd, a bell ringing … Putting all of that together, lined up end to end, made a full day, a day like any other, nothing to mark it out, the kind of day she must have experienced thousands of times before, passing without a trace, and yet this time, she wanted to soak up every tiny detail. She carried on late into the night, threading the moments together like a string of pearls. When she arrived home, she was surprised to see the lights still on at the Sudres' house.

The sound of a car pulling up roused Léa from her dozing. The Sudres parked outside the Nodes' house. Marlène was with them. They waved hello and began unloading a large number of tins, packets and bottles, along with a folded wheelchair. While Martial helped Marlène carry in her provisions, Odette crossed the road to join Léa beside the pool. She plonked herself onto a chair with a sigh. In her red polka-dot sundress, she looked rather like a deflating beach ball. She swung round to face Léa.

'Are you OK, Léa?'

'Um, fine, yes.'

'Are you sure? Nothing's happened?'

'No, nothing at all. Why? What's the matter? You seem a bit on edge …'

'It's the gypsies.'

'What gypsies?'

'Haven't you seen them? They're camped out next to the main road.'

'No … so, what about them?'

'At least nothing happened to you. That's the main thing. I'll tell you, there's been a lot going on here over the last twenty-four hours!'

Odette launched into a blow-by-blow account of the previous day's events, which had so nearly ended in tragedy: Monsieur Flesh's warning, the gypsies, the berry tart, the gunshot … The whole thing was so barmy Léa could not help but let out a snigger.

'Sorry, Odette, it's just so … absurd!'

'That may be, but Martial's still at sixes and sevens about it.'

'I'm not surprised! Maxime must be out of his mind … It's ridiculous, I've been past there twice, during the day and at night, and nothing at all has happened. I didn't even see any gypsies. And besides, what do we have to be scared of? Why on earth would they want to attack us? It's ludicrous! We live in the safest place in the whole area … Don't you agree, Odette?'

The fly must have landed on the end of Odette's nose because she was staring at it cross-eyed, screwing up her face.

'Of course, Léa, my thoughts entirely. It's nonsense … Although, when we went out shopping this morning, there were ten caravans, when there were only five yesterday, and on the way back I counted fifteen … fifteen caravans!'

'And?'

'And nothing … it's just becoming rather a lot of them.'

'Come on, Odette, it wouldn't make any difference if there

were a hundred of them. Why would they wish us any harm? And I'll say it again: the security here's enough to rival the Bank of France.'

'But that's just it! The yobs will come running if they think we've got safes to crack.'

'Not you as well, Odette, please! Maxime may have lost it, but we've got to stay calm.'

'But what about Monsieur Flesh? He knows the area …'

'Listen, to tell the truth, I'd be more likely to trust the gypsies than him. I don't like that man, there's something sly about him.'

'I'm not too fond of him either … But sometimes you need men like him around. I don't know what to think any more … In any case, you should take care, Léa. I respect your wish to be independent, but as the saying goes, there's no smoke without fire.'

She swiped the end of her nose and brought her closed fist up to her ear. She slowly loosened her fingers. There was no fly in her palm.


While Marlène piled up tins of food and bags of pasta, rice, flour and sugar on the shelves in the cellar, Maxime practised going from room to room in his wheelchair. The house's clever design meant he could get around just as easily indoors as out. The chair handled beautifully; with a bit of practice, he'd be able to get it doing some pretty nifty moves. It reminded him of his first tricycle, a red one. He had soon learnt to hurtle through the flat at breakneck speed, frantically ringing his bell. The wheel had always seemed to him to be man's greatest invention. He had racked up a few tricycles in his time, then bicycles, mopeds, motorbikes and cars ... A few accidents too, along the way ... one of them serious – for the driver he hit head-on, at least. On a road he knew like the back of his hand, ten miles from home! ... What the hell was the silly bugger doing there? ... Yes, he was going a bit fast and yes, he had had a bit to drink ... But damn it, there was never usually anyone else around! ... They had had to cut the body out of the Renault 5. Not a pretty sight, by all accounts ... He was young, the chap ... At times like that, it helps to know people in the right places. He got off with a six-month suspension and a 10,000-franc fine. His Saab had hardly a scratch on it. Bloody good motors, Saabs ... He had spotted one in *Autosport*: a smashing, top-of-the-range 4 × 4, a real tank of a car, with bull bars and tinted windows. A car like that could take on anything, which was exactly what he needed, living out here in the country ... Especially now these gypsies had turned up! ... And if they stuck around, then what? Yes, let's talk about the gypsies, shall we? The other three had taken the mickey out of him the night before, but they had certainly changed their tune this morning, coming back from the shops! They had seen with their own eyes the speed at which those gypsies were multiplying, so who was having the last laugh now?

Marlène managed to squeeze one last packet of turkey escalopes into the jam-packed freezer. There, now they were ready to face a siege. As she stood back to survey the overloaded shelves, she sang to herself: *'Et maintenant, que vais-je faire, de tout ce temps que sera ma vie?'* Go for a swim and then make lunch, that was what. It was so hot she wished she could strip off her skin. She went to the bedroom to get changed, but wasn't happy with any of the swimming costumes she tried on. It was one of those days when nothing looked right. She ran her hand over her legs. How was she going to get a wax if she couldn't go out? Those damned gypsies! ... They were awfully good-looking though, the men, women and children ... Not dirty or scruffy. The kids ran around laughing, the women hung out multicoloured laundry, the men sat chatting ... They seemed at home in the sunshine. The caravans looked roomy and well-kept, just like the Mercedes that towed them. They couldn't have paid for all that by selling baskets, that was for sure ... Maybe Maxime was right after all ... They didn't seem to mind not having walls, brazenly going about their business for all to see, as if they had nothing to hide. That was a sure sign they weren't like the rest of us; how could you feel at home wherever you went? No, they weren't normal. Yet both times she had passed them, she had stared hungrily at them with a mixture of apprehension and attraction, the same way she had felt as a little girl being taken to the zoo. Even in their cages, the animals had seemed freer than she was; they could roar, roll about, shit, piss, mate or masturbate in front of the visitors without a trace of shame. Unlike humans, the look in their eyes was clear, direct and unsullied. At the time, she had wanted to be a vet. She had started out as a *petit rat*, a young ballerina at the Paris Opéra. She liked dancing. Sometimes, when performing a leap or a twirl, she felt as graceful as a deer or a cat, sharing the same innate understanding of her body. The space belonged to her, there were no walls holding her back ... It was a feeling in her stomach, yes, around her navel, vibrating like the needle of a compass ... Like ... when Régis was born ... And never again since.

Marlène put on the first swimming costume that came to hand, a black one-piece, and stormed out of the room in a kind of rage. Maxime almost ran her over as he sprang out from the corridor at top speed.

'Where are you going?'

'Where do you think I'm going dressed like this? To mass?'

'All right, keep your hair on! What's the matter?'

'Nothing's wrong. I'm just hot. Need to go for a swim.'

'Bloody hell, someone got out of bed on the wrong side this morning! Fine, go to the pool, see if I care.'

She would have liked to slap him, just like that, for no reason at all, or maybe because he looked like a stupid, ugly bastard slumped in an old man's wheelchair.

The fly swatter struck the corner of the table with a loud thwack. Martial turned it over and presented his wife with what was left of the fly.

'That's it, gone!'

Odette peered closer, adjusting her glasses.

'That's not the one.'

'Sorry.'

'It was kind of you to try. I think I'm going to have a lie-down, this heat's knocked me out.'

It was indeed oppressive that day. The air hung stagnant, thick and muggy, not a breath of wind. Everyone felt weighed down, their every move an enormous effort. Besides killing flies in the hope of catching Odette's, there was very little to do. Martial waved the fly swatter idly before his nose. He had killed twelve since this morning and had found it surprisingly enjoyable. Martial had never been hunting, had never cut a pig's throat or bled a rabbit or wrung a chicken's neck. The only blood he had ever spilt was his own. That's not to say he had never felt the urge. Sometimes in his dreams he had let rip a little, but in dreams, anything goes. It was strange, but since Maxime had shot at him, he had become fixated on the revolver; he wanted one of his own, the same as Maxime's. Not because of the gypsies, or to defend himself from anything, no; just so that he could feel the weight of the weapon in his hand, the roughness of the grip, to hold out his arm, close one eye, cock the hammer, and then ... The target was not important. His parents, staunch pacifists and strict vegetarians, had never even let him have a pop gun, dart gun or water pistol, nor indeed anything that might in any way be seen to mimic war play or hunting. At tea time, Martial would nibble his way through his Petit Beurre biscuits so that he could go out and play with his classmates and swap his chocolate bar for slices of saucisson. The disappointment every Christmas at finding another miserable board game, Meccano No. 4 set or a light-up globe under the tree, while his friends strutted about dressed as Zorro or Robin Hood ... Wham! ... The thirteenth fly gave up its flattened ghost on the arm of the chair. Maxime blew sharply on the swatter and a speck of existence fell away.

'I don't give a damn what special powers you have and, as for your report, you know where you can stick it! My gun licence is entirely in order and if that's not enough, let me tell you I have friends in the very highest places. If you bloody well got on with your job instead of hounding good, honest people, we wouldn't have to worry about defending ourselves! For crying out loud, it's a free country, isn't it?'

Monsieur Flesh shrugged and turned on the doorstep of Maxime's house, leaving its wheelchair-bound owner beetroot-red and spitting venom. On his way out of the garden, he shoved past Martial coming the other way, having overheard the end of the argument. Something along the lines of 'stupid old fart' emerged from the caretaker's pursed lips. Martial carried on up the path, his hand outstretched.

'What's going on, Maxime?'

'Some bastard's told him I shot at you … Martial, it wasn't …'

'The very idea! I'd never dream of it, nor would Odette! We keep those sorts of things to ourselves.'

'What about Léa then?'

'She wasn't here.'

'Well, someone must have told him! … Forget it, I don't give a damn. Let's have a drink, that moron has got me all wound up.'

The umbrella kept the men in a cone of shade, like two sad clowns left in the gloomy big top at the end of the show. They could hear laughter and splashing coming from the swimming pool. Maxime was on his third glass. Beads of sweat, darkened by hair dye, streamed from his temples to his neck.

'That pool … That damned pool! There's nothing to do in this place but swim. We're not bloody ducks! … Are all three of them in there?'

'I didn't see Léa.'

'With all that coming and going, that woman's going to come to no good. It'll be her own doing.'

'Will you tell me something, Maxime? During the war, did you kill anybody?'

'Why do you want to know that?'

'I don't know, I just wondered … what it's like …'

'It's like … well, it's not like anything, because you never know. Most of the time it's dark or you're surrounded by smoke and you can't see anything. You just shoot … and maybe.'

'What about bodies? Did you ever see dead bodies?'

'Of course I did! I don't see quite what you're getting at.'

'Oh nothing. Like I said, I just wondered … I've seen dead people too, but they died naturally – my father, my mother, an uncle, an aunt … You see what I mean, it's not the same … because they were old, I suppose.'

'You're right, it's not the same. It's like they're just playing dead. It all happens so quickly in war … I've seen bodies twisted out of all recognition, blown to bits, torn apart, blackened … Could we talk about something else?'

'Yes, of course, sorry … Maxime, would you mind showing me your revolver?'

'If you like. Are you keen on guns?'

'I know nothing about them.'

Maxime took the Smith & Wesson from behind his back and held it out to Martial.

'Watch yourself, it's loaded. The safety's on, but still …'

Martial took the weapon like a relic in his outstretched palm.

'It's heavy!'

'It's the real deal. You have to know what you're doing. That's an ergonomic grip; I had it made to fit my hand. You're untouchable when you're holding it, every shot on target …'

He was interrupted by the sound of the telephone ringing. To Martial's great surprise, Maxime leapt out of his chair to answer it. While he was speaking, Martial took aim at the gate, then a bird and the window of the house across the road … Bang! Bang! Bang! …

Maxime sat back down.

'What the hell would I want a new fitted kitchen for?! … So, what do you make of it?'

'It's grand! Thanks, you can have it back now. So you're back on your feet, are you?'

'Some of the time. Let's just say I've got rather used to this chair. It suits me pretty well. We all deserve to be looked after now and then, don't we?'

'Absolutely.'

Maxime slipped the gun under the cushion behind his back and poured himself another drink, which he sipped pensively.

'It was Léa …'

'What was?'

'It was Léa who reported me to that idiot caretaker. Odette and Marlène will have filled her in – women can't help but gossip. Not that I'm surprised, coming from a dyke like her!'

'A dyke …?'

'A lesbian, in other words.'

'Are you saying Léa's …'

'That's exactly what I'm saying! I can spot them a mile off. She's been all over Marlène from the minute she arrived.'

'No! … Marlène?'

'You'd better believe it! Hands off, my girl, that's private property!'

'Léa … Well, I never! Who'd have thought it …'

'That's how it is, Martial old chap. Even here, I know, even here!'

What on earth was up with them all today? Honestly, the looks on their faces! Not even Léa could bring herself to smile. Fair enough, it was hot and sticky, there was a storm brewing, and it made your body prickle all over, but even so ... It was bad timing because Nadine had read an article earlier in the week about 'laughter therapy', a new technique devised by doctors, psychologists, yoga teachers, sophrologists, masseurs and other therapists, and today was the day she was going to try it out on the group. She had mugged up on a few physical and mental exercises designed to promote happiness, positive thinking and self-esteem, and to help things along she had baked herself a little hash cake which was beginning to kick in. The Sudres, the Nodes and Léa had listened obediently as she introduced her theme, assuring them it was scientifically proven that we should all laugh for at least fifteen minutes per day to maintain good health, upping the dose in case of illness to re-establish a virtuous circle, stimulating the immune system and ending the vicious cycle of illness, depression and weakened defences ...

For Christ's sake! There really wasn't much to it; all they

needed to do was join hands and laugh … Five pairs of eyes as cloudy as the sky stared blankly back at her. The air conditioning in the clubhouse had still not been fixed, so Nadine found herself standing in front of a row of streaming faces, like waxworks of forgotten celebrities being melted down before coming back as more contemporary figures. All in all, a disconcerting sight. Nadine's mouth was dry and her eyelids drooped as though too big for her eyes. A dull itch tickled the palms of her hands. Clearly her audience was unconvinced. They looked at the floor, avoiding her gaze, all except Maxime, who glared right at her with a face like thunder.

'Give me one thing to laugh about. Just one!'

'Well … I don't know, Maxime … Anything, it doesn't matter! … You don't have to have a reason to laugh.'

'OK, here's one for you. Here we all are, thinking we're among friends, you know, people we can trust, and the minute your back's turned, someone goes and tells all sorts of stories about you, stories that could land you in a whole heap of trouble, and then that person ever so quietly sneaks back in as though nothing ever happened. How's that for a joke, huh?'

Wedged into his chair, white-knuckled hands clutching the wheels, elbows sticking out and shoulders raised, Maxime looked like a disabled athlete poised to start a race. Marlène turned stiffly towards him, as though swivelling on a pivot.

'What on earth are you talking about, Maxime?'

'I'm telling it like it is. There's no way I'm going to sit here laughing with someone who goes blabbing behind my back, when they weren't even there!'

Nadine was beginning to wonder if that cake had been such a good idea. She was getting the most awful vibes off this man. Nothing for it but to take the snail approach and curl up within herself, praying for her guardian angel to come and rectify this casting error and take her safely home.

Marlène pressed on.

'What do you mean, Maxime? Who's saying what about whom?'

'No need to spell it out, she knows exactly who she is! If there's anyone here who needs to explain themselves, it's her.'

With the exception of Nadine, who had just closed her eyes, the women looked questioningly at each other until Léa began shaking her head with a sigh.

'Fine, I get it! If it's me you're talking about, Maxime, there's really no need for all this fuss. I was on my way out the night before last when Monsieur Flesh stopped me to give me the same rubbish about the gypsies he had spouted to Marlène. I told him it was stupid of him to scare people with stories like that and, thanks to him, there had almost been a very serious accident. I didn't say a word against you. That's all there is to it.'

'And how did you know what happened that day, when you weren't there?'

'Because Odette told me!'

'Oh, that's just great, isn't it? Just great. So now everybody's in on it! Thanks, Odette, thanks a lot!'

Odette looked as though she had been slapped round the face with a wet fish. For a few seconds, a heavy silence hung in the air, before everyone began talking over each other.

'Well, excuse me!'

'Odette, please …'

'Maxime, say you're sorry!'

'Stop it! This is ridiculous. It's all down to that idiot caretaker …'

'I wasn't talking to you …'

'Anyway, my son Régis is a lawyer, so …'

'No one said anything about pressing charges!'

'Mind your manners! Martial, say something!'

'But even if you did, Régis …'

'Marlène, will you stop banging on about Régis! He's dead, for Christ's sake! Dead! Can't you get that into your head?'

The conversation too was cut dead. It was like a henhouse after the fox has left, a few stray feathers left swirling in the air. Marlène had gone pale. Standing in the middle of the room with her hands clamped over her stomach, she seemed to be teetering on the edge of an abyss. Then she loosened up, took a deep breath and fluffed up her hair. She was smiling.

'Don't be silly, Régis isn't dead. He's absolutely fine. In fact, he sent me a tape yesterday of a piano piece he composed himself. He's a brilliant musician … I'll go and get it.'

She calmly crossed the room without catching anyone's eye, opened the door and disappeared into the blinding daylight outside.

Léa turned back to Maxime. 'I can't make out if you're a total bastard or just thick as shit.'

'Shut your mouth, you filthy dyke! Stop sticking your damned oar in!'

Suddenly he sprang out of his wheelchair and ran after his wife.

Odette was gobsmacked. 'He can walk?'

Nadine was the only one still sitting down. Of course, the story had gone right over her head, but blimey, they had acted it out brilliantly, with such conviction. She was almost tempted to break into applause.

Odette closed her clubhouse folder with a look of sadness.

'I think I'll put, "Meeting cancelled due to adverse weather". What do you say, Nadine?'

'Good idea, yes … What's all this about the gypsies?'

'Didn't you see them, by the main road?'

'Yes, but they're all over the place at this time of year. What's the problem?'

'Come with me, I'll tell you all about it. I need to get some air, even if there isn't any.'

The three women walked out, whispering. Martial sat himself down in Maxime's wheelchair. It really was comfortable, apart from the gun sticking into his back. He stayed there for a while, looking up at the ceiling where all the names that had been flung around continued to reverberate. It made his head spin …

It's going to blow up ... Everything does, sooner or later, even the star-studded sky that's nothing more than a great moth-holed curtain, drawn across to hide the mess, with that Cyclops ogling us from the other side. Lieutenant Bardu was right: 'Life is like this fucking minefield. No one gets out alive. Onward!' All that had been left of him was his shoes. So what? Can't keep it up for ever, can we? Everything's temporary, the Pyramids as well as Les Conviviales, built on shifting sand, based on guesswork. Long live death! It's what keeps us alive. Nothing to it, that's just the way it is, all goes to rust and dust. They were at each other's throats, those seniors and *senioritas*! Christ alive, they were ripping each other to shreds! The lame ducks weren't bobbing around on their pond today, no siree, they were tearing each other's feathers out, pecking and scratching ... The names they were calling each other! ... Mouthing off about anything and everything: just you wait, I'll press on your boils, your buboes, I'll show you my stump ... Doesn't bear repeating. They don't know what's in store for them. It's all wrapped up. Right about now, Dacapo and company are emptying the coffers, getting ready to take the money and run, far, far away from here, to some distant tax haven. It's bye-bye Les Conviviales! Total flop, gone bust! Open up the hatches, the rats are fleeing this sinking ship. Five years, tops, and it'll be nothing but jungle here. The monkeys will be climbing on the ruins. You only have to look at the quality of the materials: shoddy plaster slapped onto balsa-wood frames bought with rubber cheques! Why bother making it sturdy? It's only for doddery old people, on their last legs and with more money than they know what to do with. So they take it off them – it only has to look shiny and stay standing long enough for them to fill their pockets and then it's so long, suckers! … Afterwards, there'll be no one left to tell the tale. Nature will take back what's rightfully hers. Nature was what I took care of; as for the houses, I couldn't give a stuff. I like plant life, it's reliable, doesn't want to chat and wave its hands about, takes its time, grows out of sight underground and once it's taken root in the depths of hell, it breaks out and smothers everything, like an anaconda, a python, one huge muscle wrapping itself around the planet and then … crack! Enough said. Of course it was bound to go to shit, putting all these old folk in one place, but it would have been just the same if they were young. People can't help devouring one another – whether they're hungry for hate or love, it all boils down to the same thing. Doesn't bother me – I'm out of here tomorrow, heading back to Saint-Dié. I've got a lifeboat waiting for me. Let's just say I've done well out of Dacapo, so silence is golden – hand over the money and thank you, sir! I could smell trouble brewing, way back. My bags are packed. Sorry, what's that? The camera's stopped working? … Never mind, nothing to see here, carry on … I can just imagine the looks on their faces, the Sudres, the Nodes, the pretty one, Léa, and that other airhead, Nadine … I was starting to enjoy watching them squirm ... You end up getting attached, even to fuckwits like them ... They keep you company, at least ... When I get to Saint-Dié, I'm going to open my own kennels; I've already bought the land. There's a lot of money in dogs, you know. All you get from old people is gossip. No teeth left, so all they can do is dribble and lick. Good for nothing but sticking stamps on letters they'll never post. More or less useless once they're just skin and bone, down to their last drops of blood, sweat and tears. When all the liquid's gone ... What if, before I go, I, Gérard Flesh tell them they've been screwed over right from the start? ... But why should I? ... They don't like me ... and there'd be no point anyway ... We'd all just end up saying we didn't like each other, and there'd be no point in that either ... Oh, would you look at that stupid prick Martial! The man can't drive to save his life – he's reversed right into my privet hedge ...

The beam of torchlight swept over the shrub's flattened corner. Gérard Flesh knelt down and collected the broken branches. He felt a pang of hurt, like the time he threw the bouquet into the bin at ... which station was it again? ... She hadn't come ...

 'Monsieur Flesh ...?'

The humble tune, called simply 'To My Mother', had been playing on a loop in the Nodes' living room for hours. Each time the cassette ended, Marlène rewound it and set it off from the beginning again. For Maxime, this was turning into abject torture akin to the dentist's drill on a decayed tooth. How he would have loved to put on a big pair of ski boots and stamp on the damned tape!

'Marlène, you'll only upset yourself ...'

'This is my favourite bit ... And to think he taught himself ...'

'Marlène, please ...'

She didn't hear him. She had shut him out; he no longer figured in her field of vision. She hadn't reproached him, she hadn't cried, she had just set that blasted music going and barricaded herself inside it, out of reach, as smooth and devastating as a mirror.

Régis was fifteen when he composed this piece on the white piano he got for his birthday. No one could know that a year later he would die of an overdose, alone in a filthy squat around the back of the Gare de Lyon. They had not heard from him in six months. Nothing, not even a phone call or a letter. He had simply vanished into thin air, in spite of the countless attempts of police, private detectives and diviners to trace him. That's the problem with kids who don't have problems, who have always done well and apparently never wanted for anything. Maxime and Marlène had not seen it coming and had never understood why. When they had been called to the morgue to identify the body, Régis looked so different that for a split second they thought it was a mistake. So thin, with the beginnings of a beard … This faint glimmer of hope was short-lived, at least as far as Maxime was concerned – for ever since that day, even after the funeral, Marlène continued to harbour doubts in spite of all evidence to the contrary. Half of her had had to face facts, but the other half carried on day after day embroidering a glittering future for her adored son. To begin with, Maxime had been troubled by his wife's morbid fixation and had made appointments with various doctors, but it had been no use. In the end, he had come to accept the ghostly figure standing between them, even if at times, as now, he found it abhorrent.

'Marlène, I'm begging you … I've already said I'm sorry – what the hell do you want from me? Turn it off, it's driving me mad!'

'I'm not angry with you. You don't know what love is, you couldn't understand.'

'I loved Régis too, just as much as you did!'

'No, you didn't. You love cars, nice suits, material things … But you don't love people, or if you do, you love them as objects. You pick them up, play around with them, then chuck them away. You must feel very lonely sometimes …'

'No, no, I don't! How dare you tell me I haven't suffered, that I'm not still suffering? I would have given him everything! Everything!'

'Everything except what mattered. But how can you give what you don't have?'

'It's easy for you to lay all the blame on me. What was I supposed to do when I was on the road all the time? I had to be, so I could keep sending money for you to spoil him, for you to screw that poor kid up, for you to stuff all your love down his throat until he couldn't breathe! ... Cheer up. Was it something I said?'

Wrapped in their colourful satin dressing gowns, they looked like two knackered boxers. For how long had they been wearing each other down with endless fights from which neither emerged victorious, always gearing up for a rematch? The music had stopped. Marlène made no attempt to start it up again. The round was over, nil-nil. Oddly enough, it was at moments like this when they had thrown in the towel that they felt closest to one another, like two survivors in no man's land. Then they would suddenly feel the urge to throw themselves on one another and make love like animals.

The French windows leading out onto the deck were wide open but there was not the slightest breeze coming in. The huge, dense bulk of darkness let nothing through.

'I fancy a mint julep. Shall I make one for you too?'

'That would be nice.'

Maxime had just stood up when a deafening shot rang out.

'What on earth ...'

'It came from the Sudres'.'

In a split second, Maxime added it all up: gunshot + his gun hidden under the seat of the wheelchair left behind in the clubhouse + Martial's curious fascination with the weapon = ...

'Oh Jesus!'

Marlène's heeled mules slowed her down as she scurried after her husband towards the Sudres' house. Her dressing gown flapped around her skinny legs, making her look like a gigantic moth fluttering down the street.

Nadine's little red Clio had categorically refused to start. It had broken down on her before, but judging by the large puddle of oil on the ground beneath the engine, it seemed to have made its mind up this time. Léa had offered to let her come back to her place and call out a mechanic, but Nadine was not keen. Getting a breakdown truck to come out here would cost a fortune. But her old friend Gilbert, who always knew how to get her going again (in more ways than one), could easily tow away the wreck with his Land Rover. Unfortunately, she had to make do with leaving a message on his answering machine, asking him to call her back as soon as possible on Léa's number. There was nothing for it but to wait, a discipline she had been well trained in over the years. Léa had poured them cold drinks, which they now sipped in silence. They were hitting the spot, but the mood remained subdued.

'What a mess! And all over nothing ... I really don't get this whole thing with the gypsies. It's just such a load of balls! Sorry, Léa, but there's no other way to describe it.'

'It's the only word for it. We'll have trouble breathing the same air now. There wasn't much of it to go round to start with ... Right from day one, I've felt like I was living under a bell jar here – do you know what I mean?'

'Absolutely. A big glass cloche, like the ones you put over melons.'

'Exactly ... A glass trap.'

'Why don't you get out of here, Léa? Who cares about the house? You'll find something else. I know of a few places up for rent around here, can't be any worse ...'

'You're right, that's what I should do ... only, I don't think I will.'

'Why not?'

'Because for me, this is where it's going to happen.'

'Where what's going to happen?'

'I don't know ... I've just got a feeling about it, something important. It's hard to explain, it's just knowing that there's a kind of ... logic to it all ...You know, many years ago, when I was four or five, my mother lost me at a market. I was all alone in a forest of moving people, their legs cutting across me like scissors every way I turned. At first I was scared, short of breath, frozen with panic at having no hand to guide me ... and then suddenly it struck me that, in fact, I was right where I was supposed to be. How can I describe it? I was like a stone at the side of a road; I stopped asking questions, I was just there. I remember it very clearly, that feeling of certainty, of total belief ... Didn't stop me spending the rest of my life wondering what the hell I was doing here ... Oh, it's raining.'

A few drops spattered down on the dusty ground, warm and heavy, slow enough to count. It made you want to ask the sky, 'Is that all you've got to show for yourself?', as the clouds slunk away.

'Gilbert still hasn't called me back ... I'm sorry.'

'Let's wait a while longer and if we don't hear from him, I'll take you home.'

'Oh no, you won't! It's a long way. And then there are the gypsies ...'

'Oh please, not you as well! Otherwise, you'll just have to stay the night here. Unless Maxime's "revelations" have put you off me ...?'

'I couldn't care less; it doesn't bother me in the slightest. Whatever makes you happy.'

'Do you like opera? *Madame Butterfly*?'

Maria Callas's voice rose and fell like water spurting from a fountain. The temperature had not changed; it was still just as hot, the air just as static. The moon had now appeared, right in the middle of the sky. Suddenly a loud bang blew it to smithereens. Nadine and Léa got up off their loungers in unison, each as pale as the other.

'Was that a gun?'

'I don't know ... It came from the Sudres'.'

All things considered, you could get on just fine with a fly. You only had to rub along together and lay out ground rules that suited you both. Not that you had much choice in the matter ... Now, for example, the fly must be asleep. Thus, in order to avoid disturbing it, Odette tried to make as little movement as possible. Why was it so difficult to live together? Why did you always have to pick sides? Why had they all started laying into each other? The scene at the clubhouse had left a shameful taste in her mouth, something obscene and indecent she could not get rid of. People turn stupid and ugly when they're angry, even Léa ... So what if Léa liked women? ... A manager she had shared an office with for twenty years was one of them too, and it had never been an issue. We all have our weaknesses ... Martial had not stopped grinding his teeth all evening. The day's events seemed to have knocked him sideways, perhaps even more than her. 'I'm going for a walk'; he had barely touched his dinner. He's a sensitive soul, Martial, he doesn't give anything away, bottles it all up inside … 'The Mystery of the Ministry', his colleagues used to call him. Perhaps the two of them needed to get away for a few days … Even when you spent your whole life on holiday, you were still entitled to a break now and then! … Maybe they could go up to the mountains; it would be cooler there … Take a step back, see the bigger picture …

A gunshot doesn't sound like a tyre bursting or a firework going off. It's in the silence that follows that you begin to gauge the gravity of it. Odette had the impression it was the moon that had been fired at; she saw it quivering like a gong, right in the middle of the sky. It came from just behind the house … the way Martial had gone …

Monsieur Flesh looked like a starfish washed ashore, arms and legs outstretched and his face reduced to a blood-spattered sketch. The bullet had ripped out his right eyeball which now lay half a metre from his head, staring up at the moon from the freshly mown lawn. A big white marble. Mashed-up face aside, Monsieur Flesh did not look dead; it was as though an echo of life was left in him. Martial would not have been surprised to see him get up, pick up his eye and put it back in place, grumbling as he went. But he didn't get up. The revolver at the end of his arm was heavy and searing hot against his thigh. Martial felt incredibly serene, at peace. If the others had not descended on him practically all at once, crowding in on him, he would have happily gone to bed. Maxime snatched the gun from his hand and began circling the caretaker's body, flapping his arms up and down as though trying to fly away.

'Oh, Jesus! ... And with my gun as well! ... You fucking idiot! Why the hell did you do it?'

It was the first time Maxime had sworn at him, and Martial felt a certain sense of achievement. Nadine bent over and began vomiting. Léa had turned into a pillar of salt, utterly white, while Marlène was hiding her face in her hands, letting out little mouse-like squeaks. Odette opened and closed her mouth, unable to produce the slightest sound, flailing about hopelessly like a person drowning. The moon had returned to its quarters and averted its gaze, displaying complete disinterest in this clutch of homunculi. Maxime came and stood squarely in front of Martial.

'Come on, why did you do it, you stupid bastard? Why?'

'I don't know. It just happened ... It wasn't me ...'

'It wasn't you?! Well, who the hell was it then? Of course it was bloody you! And with my gun!'

Odette placed herself between Maxime and her husband.

'You mustn't talk to him like that, Maxime. Martial's very sensitive ...'

'Oh please, Odette, I think the time for niceties is past! In case you hadn't noticed, there's a dead man lying in front of us! But no, everything's just hunky-dory!'

Léa stepped towards Martial and Odette, who now formed one inseparable bloc.

'How are you feeling, Martial?'

'OK ... Yes, OK, I think ... He was there, by the hedge. I held my arm out towards him, I said, "Monsieur Flesh ..." It went off

… My whole arm shook, the shot rang out and I saw him almost lifted off the ground … It was the gun, you see, it wasn't me …'

'We'll have to call the police.'

Maxime stepped in, pouring with sweat.

'The police? Are you mad?!'

'We have to!'

'Wait, it was *my* gun he fired. Do you have any idea what that means? Anyway, it was an accident. Martial clearly isn't in his right mind.'

'But … what else do you suggest we do?'

Odette clung to her husband, nervously muttering over and over, 'Not the police! Not the police! Not prison …' Nadine was sitting on the ground, rubbing her temples as she rocked back and forth, eyes closed. Marlène had crouched at her side like a frightened little poodle.

Maxime went on, 'All we have to do is hide the body. Just get rid of it somewhere.'

'Have you completely lost it? And where do you suggest we do that?!'

'Behind the gypsy camp, in that patch of scrubland.'

'But … that's … You can't be serious!'

'Just think about it for a second, Léa. What do you want to do, tear Odette and Martial's life apart and ruin ours while you're at it? Say "to hell with it all"? You could never stand the man anyway. Why should you give a toss? We're the only witnesses and as long as we keep our mouths shut, no one's going to come sniffing around a bunch of poor old pensioners minding their own business. Martial, are you up to this? Say something, damn it, it's your neck on the line!'

The truth was Martial no longer felt he had anything to do with all this. The moonlight was amazing; everyone and everything seemed to have been chalked up on a blackboard. Any minute it could all be rubbed off … Odette began shaking him like a rag doll.

'He's right, darling. We have to do as Maxime says. Afterwards we won't have to think about it ever again; we just need to do this one little thing … No, no, you're not going to prison … How should we do this, Maxime?'

'We're going to need a tarpaulin or some bin bags to wrap around the head. Then we stick him in the boot and chuck him out over there, in the rubble, and no one's any the wiser. It's watertight. No one will suspect us for a minute … As long as we keep this between ourselves, that is. We have to be sure we can trust each other. Isn't that right, Léa?'

Léa let it go. This man was one of life's irredeemable idiots, the kind that always have to have the last word. Odette had already made up her mind which side to take. Marlène would be bound to follow suit. As for Nadine …

'Nadine?'

'I don't give a shit! Do what the hell you like; you're all completely messed up. I should never have set foot in this place. I've seen nothing, heard nothing, I just want to go home.'

Léa shrugged her shoulders; Maxime puffed out his chest.

'Since we're all agreed, what are we waiting for?'

Odette and Maxime got on with the job with remarkable efficiency. Martial, on the other hand, was incapable of taking the slightest initiative and simply did as he was told. The three other women stood motionless, silently watching the operation unfold. Once the body had been bundled up and crammed into the boot, Maxime got behind the wheel while Martial and Odette leant against one another in the back. Léa, Nadine and Marlène stepped back to let the car turn round, then watched it take off down the road and disappear into the night. Léa shook her head with a sigh.

'This is utter madness ... Come on, Marlène, we can all wait together at my place. Nadine, are you coming? What is it?'

Nadine was pointing at a corner of the lawn. Monsieur Flesh's right eye lay untroubled, carrying on its staring contest with the moon.


The car came back a good three-quarters of an hour later. The three women awaiting its return – one biting her nails and staring into space, another making gallons of tea nobody wanted to drink and the third sucking a hastily rolled spliff in the bathroom – hurried out to see it pulling up outside the Sudres'. Martial still seemed to be away with the fairies. He was smiling like a village idiot, which jarred with the crestfallen looks on Maxime's and Odette's faces. Marlène leapt towards her husband.

'Is it over then?'

'No ... we couldn't do it.'

'But ... I thought you said it was the best thing to do?'

'I didn't say we'd changed our minds! We just couldn't do it. Just before we reached the camp, I turned down a track on the left, heading towards that dumping ground. Obviously I had switched my lights off. At the end of the track, there was a big heap of rubble. It seemed like a suitable place to do it. I tried to turn the car round so that we'd be ready to go as soon as we were finished, only ... while I was reversing, the back wheel got stuck in a rut, in a hole I hadn't seen. Martial and I tried as hard as we could to push the car out, but there was no shifting it ...'

'So, how did you do it?'

Maxime hunched his shoulders, dug his hands into his dressing-gown pockets and kicked the tyre angrily. It was Odette who replied.

'The gypsies ... We couldn't just stand there. Who else could we ask for help? They were a bit taken aback at first, and then they started giggling. The whole lot of them came over, women, children ... so much noise, so much laughter! In no time at all they had us back on all four wheels, without expecting anything in return. It just goes to show, the things people say about them ... Well ... Anyway, then we came back here.'

'Does that mean "he" is still in the boot?'

'Well, obviously!'

All six of them stared in solemn silence at the Sudres' car, which now served as a hearse. Nadine burst out laughing. The sense she had got of driving into a cemetery on her first visit to Les Conviviales had been spot on after all. Maxime glared at her.

'Think this is funny, do you?'

'I'm sorry, it's a nervous thing. What are you going to do now?'

Of course no one was able to answer such an elementary and awkward question. Since they were now back where they had started, Léa had another go at making them see sense.

'Listen, I think it's time to stop this madness before we make things even worse. What we need to do is call the police, tell them the truth, explain how the caretaker got everyone worked up with his potty ideas about the gypsies, that Martial panicked when he heard something behind his house, it was dark ... You'd have a very good case; there are mitigating factors. The longer you leave it, the more trouble you'll find yourselves in, believe me!'

Besides Léa, no one was capable of thinking straight: Nadine because she was so spaced out she could no longer tell fact from fiction, and the other four because, quite simply, they were old, physically and mentally exhausted, and all they wanted to do was go to bed and forget all about it. Marlène was absent-mindedly bouncing a little ball of tissue in her hand, which succeeded in driving her husband to distraction.

'Will you stop throwing that thing around? What is it, anyway?'

'Monsieur Flesh's eye. You left it on the grass. I picked it up in case—'

'Go and throw it away this minute, for crying out loud! It's revolting!'

'I was only trying to help … If Régis was here, he'd know what to do. He'd know exactly what to do …'

Marlène disappeared off towards her house, humming the tune of 'To My Mother'. Maxime ran his hand over his face and then looked at his open palm, as though expecting to see his features imprinted on it. Martial was counting the stars, but kept missing one and having to start again. Odette edged towards the car boot, her nostrils quivering.

'He stinks! … He's starting to stink! We have to get him out of our car, right this instant. I can't stand the sight of him! I can't stand the smell!'

Her eyes were popping out of her head. It was no longer just one fly buzzing around her but hundreds, thousands that she batted away, waving her arms about. Léa tried to calm her down by placing a hand on her shoulder, but Odette broke away sharply as though recoiling from red-hot metal.

'Don't you touch me! All you can think about is the police. You don't have a husband, you don't know what it's like; you couldn't care less if he gets sent to die in jail! ... It's no surprise – you only like women anyway!'

This harsh and unexpected reaction gave Maxime the upper hand. He didn't really give a hoot whether Martial ended his sorry days behind bars, but purely to annoy Léa and avoid losing face, he took it upon himself to act as Odette's protector.

'It'll all be fine, Odette. I'm here, and *I* won't let you down. Here's what we're going to do. We're going to get him out of the boot and then ... then we're going to stick him in the freezer in the clubhouse – there's plenty of room in there. That will buy us time to find somewhere better. OK?'

'Yes, Maxime, good idea! At least that gives us a bit more time to play with ... Let's go!'

Léa saw there was no point putting up a fight.

'You're completely out of your minds. More fool you. You can rest assured I won't report you, but don't expect me to get involved in your ghoulish antics.'

'We don't need you anyway, do we, Maxime?'

'Not in the slightest. Go and open up the clubhouse please, Odette. I'll move the car over.'

A warm breeze had picked up. It was like being under a hairdryer. Nadine thought she might have her hair cut very short and dye it red.

'How many fingers am I holding up, Léa? ... How many?'

Who was this girl putting on a puppet show under her nose?

'How many fingers, Léa?'

A hundred and fifty? Maybe a few less? It was hard to say; she was waving her hands about so quickly they looked like fans. She plucked a number out of thin air.

'Ten.'

'Ten! Yes, ten! Oh, Léa, you had me worried there.'

It was light outside. Nadine ... What was she doing here?

'What time is it?'

'Nine o'clock in the morning. Are you OK? Do you feel all right?'

'I think ... I'd like an orange juice.'

'Coming right up! Léa, you know ... No, nothing. I'll go and get you a drink.'

Nadine ... Ah, yes, the broken-down car ... So she had spent the night here? ... But where had the night gone? ... How had darkness turned into daylight? ... So many times she'd been told to plan for her retirement, but no one said a word about planning for the nights ... How they drag when you get old, your sleep as restless as your shaky hands ... Her memory of the night before was like a jumpy series of black and white images, jumbled frames from an old Charlie Chaplin film: the moon, a corpse, the moon, a car starting, the moon, a cluster of dazed, dishevelled old people, the moon ... It made no sense at all ... And then there were the oysters, yes, that's right, she had fancied some oysters, had opened some ... Or rather, had tried to ... As she attempted to get up from the sofa she had been lying on, Léa felt a sharp pain in her left hand. It was wrapped in a bandage. A red star-shaped stain had seeped through the gauze. Nadine returned dressed in a baggy T-shirt, carrying the breakfast tray. There was no trace of anxiety on her face; rather she looked relieved, as though she had just been told she didn't have cancer.

'Here's some orange juice, tea ...'

'Did you sleep here last night?'

'"Sleep" might be stretching it ... but yes, I was here.'

'Still not heard from your mechanic friend?'

'No. Never mind, we'll sort it out later.'

'What's wrong with my hand?'

Nadine waved hers evasively and poured the tea. Léa pressed her.

'What did I do to it?'

'You wanted to open some oysters ... Only they were actually pebbles. You hurt yourself with the knife. It's not too bad. I dressed it for you.'

'Thank you.'

Nadine offered her the piece of toast she had just buttered. It felt good to bite into something. Her jaw was stiff, as though it had been locked around some long-kept secret. She said 'Thank you' again. The wind lifted a corner of the tablecloth; it was still just as warm. Everything more than a metre above ground was at its mercy.

'It's weird, this wind … Where's it coming from?'

'From the south. We've got at least three days of it to come.'

'Oh … Everything's so dry … It's all cracking apart.'

'Drink your orange juice.'

'What about the others? Aren't they up yet?'

'I haven't seen anyone, thank goodness. They give me the creeps.'

'Do I, too?'

'No, it's different with you.'

'I'll just have a shower and then I'll run you home.'

'It can wait … it can wait. I'm not in any hurry; there's plenty of time. I like being here, with you …'

Nadine blushed like a little girl and tried to hide it by plaiting a few tangled strands of hair in front of her face.

'Nadine … did something happen between us last night?'

'Of course not! You want to know what happened next? You … You went into your own world for a while, like you did the other day. I looked after you and you went to sleep, that's all.'

'Ah … so I went off my rocker then.'

'Don't be so dramatic! Everything's just fine. Other than trying to cut open pebbles, you didn't do anything strange. These things happen.'

'Did you undress me …?'

'I had to, you had blood all over your dress.'

'Ah …'


While the others were busy freezing Monsieur Flesh in the clubhouse, Nadine had gone home with Léa. She was still wondering what hair colour to go for: red, but perhaps more of an aubergine shade. There was no message from Gilbert on the answering machine. Léa had put on some Billie Holliday. Like the night itself, it was so beautiful it brought tears to Nadine's eyes. Léa had opened a bottle of Lacrima Christi and as they sipped it they made light chitchat, which the breeze swiftly carried off into the darkness. When 'Strange Fruit' came on, Léa stood up and disappeared into the kitchen. A scream followed by the sound of smashing crockery roused Nadine from her comatose nirvana. The drops of blood trickling from Léa's hand made little crimson suns as they splashed onto the white flagstones. She sat expressionless as her hand was bandaged, as though the whole thing had nothing to do with her. The wound was superficial; the knife had slipped on a stone. More pebbles had been arranged in a spiral on a metal tray, decorated with lemon wedges. Nadine laid Léa on the sofa, took off her bloodstained dress and put a satin dressing gown around her. She was asleep, or pretending – it was hard to tell. Nadine had had her share of sapphic experiences along with everyone else at boarding school, then later in the commune, yet it was something other than desire she felt for the languid body which lay available to her: the irresistible urge to *be* the other, from the ends of her hair to the tips of her toes, the urge to be bound together so totally that she could forget herself. Just as Nadine was wrapping the dressing gown around her, Léa grabbed her hands and held them against her breasts. A heart was beating underneath and, in that moment, the whole world seemed to throb to the same rhythm. Nadine had not left her side all night.

'Is someone cooking a barbecue?'

'I'm sorry?'

'It smells like charcoal, don't you think?'

'Yes, it does a bit …'

'Bit odd, at this time of the morning ... You know, Nadine, I still feel like oysters.'


Maxime was stroking Marlène's hair and staring up at the ceiling, which was slashed with diagonal streaks of light. It had been years since he had woken to feel the weight of her head on his chest. She had slept in his arms. Though he urgently needed to pee, he dared not move for fear of breaking this fragile moment which carried him way back in time ... a cool, bright April morning. They were cycling in the countryside. They had known each other barely a week. A friend had dragged him along to the Opéra one night and, while looking for an excuse to get out of the place before dying of boredom, he had spotted her among the corps de ballet. There were other dancers more beautiful, more brilliant, more graceful, but she was the one ... While they were laughing at one of his hilarious jokes, she had brushed against a mossy wall and fallen onto the dew-covered grass. Her knee was grazed. He licked it clean before tying his handkerchief around it. She was so beautiful! ... For the first and only time in his life, he meant everything he said. He still held out hope of becoming a racing driver, he still cherished good-quality dreams. So where had it all gone wrong? The day he married Marlène, another man had taken his place. A puffed-up, power-hungry arsehole who thought he could gobble up the whole world with his toothy Colgate smile, who had locked his pretty bird inside a cage and shelved his dreams. So he had begun selling greenhouses, and more greenhouses, sealed up nicely, taking them anywhere and everywhere, and business was good! ... Here comes golden balls! ... They don't half get in the way, though, golden balls ... He had to find a way to be shot of his load ... One-night stands in provincial hotels, each more forgettable than the last ... Every time he would come home spent, broken, exhausted, laying before his little bird an offering grabbed at the station or picked up in duty-free ... The bird would take one look at the Hermès headscarf and go back to preening her feathers. When Régis was born, he thought ... Too late, the little chick had hidden under his mother's wing, never to come out again. How had life passed him by so completely? What a waste! With all the things they cook up nowadays, shouldn't it be possible to go back in time and rub it all out with a magic eraser? ... What the hell had he got himself into last night? Why should he care what happened to the caretaker, or Martial? Life imprisonment was a pretty short sentence, at his age ... But no, the dickhead with the big horsey teeth couldn't help barging in, just to piss Léa off. He wasn't even angry she had turned him down; he actually quite liked her ... That's pride for you ... Now what were they going to do with that idiot Flesh's body? The bastard's life had not been worth a thing, but now he was dead, it had suddenly taken on a significance out of all proportion. Acid? Quicklime? Fire? The damned fool should never have been born. Marlène yawned and stretched out like a cat beside him.

'Have you made toast?'

'No.'

'Oh, I thought I could smell burning ... I'm hungry, Maxime.'

'I'll make breakfast.'

As he slipped out of bed, Marlène propped herself up on her elbow and opened one bleary eye.

'You're going to make breakfast ...?'

'Why not?'

'Are you all right?'

'Yes, I'm fine. Go back to sleep.'

His mouth tasted gamey, rotten, like a corpse. He had not brushed his teeth before bed, which was very unlike him. As he worked the toothpaste into a lather over his gums, he caught sight of his natural hair colour in the mirror. Horrified, he picked up a pair of nail scissors and began cutting into it until only half a centimetre remained. Then slowly, carefully, he shaved it all off, without leaving a trace of fluff behind. Aesthetically speaking, the result was seriously questionable, but he felt clean, clean inside. Afterwards, he went into the kitchen and made tea and coffee. The wind carried the whiff of the funeral pyre on its breath and the sky was tinged sulphurous yellow. He heard Marlène's voice from the bedroom.

'Maxime? Can't you smell it? The toast's burning!'

He had not even put the bread in the toaster.

'Have I never told you about that little girl Nicole? It was a long time ago … a long time … On the Côte d'Opale, in Wissant. It was that thing on the telly the other day that made me think of her, you know, the beast in the dunes. It was in the school holidays, we must have been six or seven … Nicole was very pretty, we got on well … One day, in the dunes, I was suddenly desperate to touch her breasts, her buttocks, her genitals. It was like a fever, and she seemed to have caught it too. We rolled around in the sand but didn't dare touch one another, catch one another. It was like we had gone mad … Then we found this little injured bird – one of its wings was broken. I could feel it pulsing in the palm of my hand; it was like holding my own heart. It looked at me with its big round eye, huge in comparison to its body.

'"If you kill it, I'll let you touch my breasts."

'Nicole muttered the words without looking at me. The wind lifted her hair, revealing her ear, which was bright red, almost glowing. I tightened my fist. I thought I heard a little "pop!" like when you squeeze bubble wrap between finger and thumb ... Yes, pop! ... I gently opened my hand ... The bird had stopped moving, its legs were stiff, it was just an object ...

'"Murderer!"

'Nicole slapped me and ran off as fast as she could. I never saw her again ... These things stay with you ... Who knows why.'

A kind of low murmur carried Martial's voice long into the silence. It was like an orchestra tuning up far, far away. Martial and Odette were lying naked on the bed, like two recumbent tomb effigies. The sheets, pushed down to the bottom of the bed, seemed sculpted from marble. It was hot like an oven.

'I should have said "no" to Nicole ... But I've never been good at saying "no". It's so much easier to say "yes" to everything! ... I think Monsieur Flesh said "yes" when he turned towards me ... You know, I didn't mean to kill the poor guy; it was the weapon in my hand that made me feel like I could finally touch the untouchable – it was incredible! I only wanted to touch him, just touch him, that's all ...'

Martial hauled himself up on his elbow. Odette's cyanotic face was turned towards him and she stared at him open-mouthed, her eyes opaque with a bluish film. A fly landed on her lip. Martial shooed it away with the back of his hand and then stood up and went into the kitchen. The fly immediately reclaimed its spot.

He opened the fridge and crouched down in front of it. What had they come down south for? He poured himself a large glass of orange juice and went out onto the deck to drink it, still dressed as nature intended. The sky was the greyish yellow of mustard gas and the air was thick with an acrid smoke that got up your nose and made your eyes prickle. Every now and then a tawny flicker could be seen in the distance. Suddenly feeling the irresistible urge to bathe, Martial headed towards the pool. He didn't feel the gravel digging into the soles of his feet. He could have walked over hot coals, he felt nothing any more.

Outside the clubhouse, he found Maxime perched on a low wall, his dressing gown flapping in the wind. He was holding his head in his hands and gabbling incomprehensibly. Martial sat down beside him.

'Morning, Maxime.'

'Martial … Jesus, it's all going up in smoke!'

'Ah, a fire.'

'We need to get the hell out of here, right this minute! You should go home and gather up anything precious and … Hang on, what are you doing walking around starkers?'

'I'm going for a dip. This heat is just …'

'A dip! That fire is heading for us like a steam train. We don't have a moment to lose. Can't you smell it?'

'What have you done to your hair?'

'My what? … Who gives a shit! Go and get Odette. Go on, go!'

'She's asleep. I don't want to wake her.'

Maxime's dressing gown hung wide open. He too was naked underneath. An ordinary man, thought Martial. Maxime looked like he was about to say something, then thought better of it. He made a gesture with his arm as though throwing a crumpled-up ball of paper over his shoulder, then jumped down from the wall and ran off towards his house. Martial climbed calmly down the metal steps. The water was lovely.

'Take what you can and scram! The fire's at the bottom of the hill.'

'We should warn Martial and Odette …'

'I've just left Martial by the pool. He's going for a swim! He's completely lost it, but what am I supposed to do about it? Just get the hell out; in half an hour the whole place is going to go up in flames. Excuse me, must be off.'

Maxime left Nadine and Léa, whom he had just run into on the street, and hurried home.

'Marlène, get up! Pack your bags, we're leaving, there's a fire.'

'A fire? … What have you done to your hair?'

'To hell with my hair! Get a bloody move on. Bring the bare minimum, there's not a minute to lose!'

While Maxime was emptying paperwork out of the drawers and cramming it into a briefcase, Marlène stood staring into her cupboard, unable to pick out a single thing. What was important? What was not? None of this made sense. How could you fit an entire life in a suitcase? And what about Régis's piano, the white piano?

'Why are you standing there like a bloody lemon? Get a wiggle on! Your jewellery, you mustn't forget your jewellery!'

'What about the others, the Sudres, Léa?'

'I've warned them, now it's up to them. Every man for himself. Right, are you ready?'


It was Nadine who took care of everything, as Léa had gone into her own world again. Maxime was right, the sky had become a blazing inferno. Charred fragments swirled in the air, which was becoming difficult to breathe. She had not even tried asking Léa to choose what to take, so was now stuffing a bag with whatever came to hand. Sitting on the edge of the sofa, Léa was frowning as though trying to remember something, while nervously playing with her fingers.

'Léa, where's your handbag? Léa, please, where's your bag? I need the car keys. Léa? ... Ah, there it is! Come on, Léa, come with me. Let's go.'

She obediently let herself be taken by the hand and led out to the car. Thick plumes of black smoke rose in the sky, where birds flew disoriented in every direction. It was no longer a murmur they could hear but a roar, a fusion of crackling and sizzling. Nadine stalled three times before starting the engine. Léa turned to her, her face a vision of calm.

'Are we going home then?'

'That's right, Léa, let's go.'

Maxime's car hurtled past them. Marlène was wearing a fur coat.


Martial was contemplating Archimedes' principle as he lay on his back, arms and legs spread wide, looking up at a sky the same flaming orange as the *Gone with the Wind* poster. With his ears underwater, he heard none of the fire's racket. It was a spectacular sight. Odette would have liked it ... Despite her sleeping pills she had been up crying all night, the kind of sobbing that breaks your heart. 'It's over, it's over ...' she said again and again ... In the small hours of the morning, she finally fell asleep. Martial had pressed the pillow over her face. She had hardly put up a fight ... She too must be floating somewhere now ...

'Damned piece of junk!'

Maxime chucked the useless remote control into the glove compartment and stormed out of the car. Nadine and Léa were waiting in the car behind. The gate stubbornly remained closed. Nadine got out to join Maxime, who was trying to yank it open. She had a go with Léa's remote control, to no avail.

'Fucking hell, we're trapped in here like damned rats! The electrics must have blown ... There's nothing for it, we'll have to climb over this bloody gate ...'

'And then what? Look around, Maxime, it's coming from every side; there's no way we'll make it on foot.'

'Well, what else are we going to do? In quarter of an hour, it's all going to blow up.'

'We'll have to go back to the pool and wait for help to arrive. That's all we can do.'

Wearing any old clothes, their faces speckled with soot, dragging their sorry suitcases behind them, they looked like a group of refugees, survivors of a nameless war. They huddled together beside the pool in which Martial floated indifferently, like flotsam. Raging uncontrollably, the flames were now licking above the level of the rooftops. The fire could be no more than a hundred metres from the perimeter wall. They had all lost the ability to speak, even to think. This was hell, the way it's painted on church walls ... The heat became so unbearable they all dived like frogs into the little turquoise rectangle set with a cluster of rubies. This was how the pilot of the water bomber flying overhead saw it.

Maxime held out his arm.

'A helicopter! The firemen can't be far behind … Everybody wave! Hey, over here! Over here!'

They all began shouting and waving their arms about – all except Martial, who was floating face down, offering his saggy white posterior to the fury of the heavens. Not that anybody took any notice. An explosion had just come from near the entrance to Les Conviviales. Gas? White-hot shards of metal, glass and wood were thrown up into the air, landing dangerously close to them. In her drenched fur coat, Marlène looked like an otter gnawing on her necklace. Having tugged it this way and that it eventually snapped, leaving one hundred and forty pink pearls strewn over the bottom of the pool.

'Oh God! Oh God! We're going to boil alive in here, Maxime!'

'Calm down, Marlène. I'm here, the firemen—'

Another explosion, closer this time and followed by a spray of sparks, made them all wince.

'It's the Sudres' house! … Odette? … Martial, it's your house! Martial …'

Maxime pulled his neighbour's body towards him and lifted his head above water.

'He's only gone and bloody drowned! … He's drowned …'

A torrent of unidentifiable debris rained down on them, some of it plunging straight to the bottom, other bits left hissing on the surface … Then came the sound of an engine and the sight of the first fireman scuttling towards them like a giant beetle. The mask over his face meant they couldn't understand a word of what he said, peering over them from the poolside. They just looked up at him wide-eyed, as though he were some kind of Martian whose language they could not speak. After lifting his visor, he managed to explain that a helicopter was on its way to airlift them to safety, since the roads were impassable.

'It'll be here in a couple of minutes. Don't worry, it's going to be all right. You're all here, there's no one left inside the houses?'

They all thought of Odette, but no one said anything.

The fireman carried on, pointing his big glove towards Martial, 'What about the gentleman over there …?'

Léa was holding Martial's head above the water but his pinched nostrils, open mouth and dull stare left little doubt as to his condition.

Léa calmly replied, 'He's drowned. His name was Martial … Yes, that's right, Martial … Martial and Odette.'

The helicopter blades began to whip up the smoke above their heads and form concentric waves on the surface of the water. A harness attached to a rope came spinning down. The fireman helped Marlène and Léa to get in. Maxime and Nadine watched them rising slowly above them. It was like a bad special effect. Then it was their turn. Once they were all squashed together inside the glass bubble, with the engine roaring, they looked down at the fireman hauling Martial's body ashore before giving the pilot the signal to leave. Down below, everything became ridiculously small.

Also by Pascal Garnier:

*The Panda Theory*
*How's the Pain?*
*The A26*